Stranded on
Castaway Island

STRANDED ON
CASTAWAY ISLAND

AMY C. LAUNDRIE

Three
Towers
Press

Milwaukee, Wisconsin

Published by
Three Towers Press
An imprint of HenschelHAUS Publishing, Inc.
www.henschelHAUSbooks.com

ISBN: 978159598-893-5
E-ISBN: 978159598-894-2
LCCN: 2022931787

Cover art and illustrations by Olena Georg

Printed in the United States of America

Dedication

To all those who support developing writers.
Many people gave freely of their time
and talents to help bring Annie, Mirra,
the mysterious footprint-maker,
and Sea Stallion to life.

ACKNOWLEDGEMENTS

My deepest appreciation to the many people (last count was 87) who contributed to *Stranded on Castaway Island,* including Gayle Rosengren and past and present members of critique groups *Writer Chicks on the Road, Twisted Willow, Newberies,* and *Women in Motion.*

I'm also immensely grateful to Frank Laundrie, Jeff Braatz, Patti Notes, Laurie Rosengren, Lisa Lickel, Joan Bauer, Cynthia Schumerth, Kristin Rens Daly, Valerie Biel, Sandy Brehl, Heather Sherry, Maria Laundrie, Emily Kokie, Susan Casper, Ann Angel, Sheri Sinykin, Sofia Jarvis, Ann Longenbach, Brian J. O' Keefe, Zoe Lucas, Kira Henschel, and Olena Georg.

It truly does take a village.

CHAPTER ONE
RED SKY

I lifted the silver and turquoise hair clip out of its special box and cradled it in the palm of my hand. A soft ache tightened my throat, the same feeling I got every time I remembered Mom's words when she had given it to me on my last birthday. "Fourteen years old. You're growing up so fast, Annie. Just don't be in a hurry to leave us."

I swept my sun-streaked hair off my neck, piled it on top of my head with a twist, and fastened the clip. I hadn't known that Mom would be the one to leave.

"Annie!" My brother's voice startled me back to reality. "Are you daydreaming again?" Joey poked his head in my bedroom. "You promised!"

I blinked. After supper, Joey had asked if he could show me something on the computer. "Be right there," I called. I undid my hair and set the clip on the dresser. Someday, I vowed. Someday I'll be more than a daughter and a big sister needing to keep the family together and more than a girl who had lost her best friend.

I picked up dirty clothes, started a load, and then joined Joey at the computer desk.

"Annie," Joey wiggled with excitement, "I went on the Humane Society website. They got in a litter of puppies, half Cocker and half Poodle." He pointed to a black and white one. "I like this one. If I can get it, I'm gonna name it Patches." He looked at me.

It hurt to see the raw want in his eyes and to hear his pleading voice.

When I didn't answer right away, Joey swallowed, his eyes brimming with tears. "Will you help me talk to Dad? I don't want to go through summer without ... you know."

Yes, I did know.

"Sure, Bug." I squeezed him close. "How about you and I talk strategy tomorrow, then ask him at lunch? It's pretty late to bring it up tonight."

"Okay." Joey grinned.

The screen door closed with a bang and Dad called, "Where is everyone?"

"In here," I said.

My fifteen-year-old cousin, Ryan, followed my dad into the bedroom. Ryan had my same green eyes, but his hair was darker than mine. "Hey, Annie," he asked, "want to walk out on the pier with me?"

Dad's rule was no walking off by ourselves at night. Ryan gave me his irresistible grin. "Yeah, sure," I said.

"Let's you and me make some popcorn," Dad said to Joey. "Steven's finishing up in the garage."

Steven, twelve, must be messing with the lawn mower again.

I grabbed a jacket, knowing how chilly it got in June after sunset along the coast of Maine. "What's up?" I asked Ryan. "You want to check out the boats?"

"I wouldn't mind." There was that irresistible Ryan-grin again.

We walked side by side across the road, passing other cottages like ours, first built as summer homes but ending up being used all year. I purposely didn't look off to the left where Mirra, my ex-best friend, lived. Her house was much grander than my family's, but that wasn't the reason I averted my eyes. I worried I'd see her out on the deck with her new best friend.

The sand was packed enough that walking was easy. A flock of gulls called as they flew off.

We walked toward the dock where a dozen or so boats bobbed in the waves. "If Steven were out there tonight," Ryan said, "he'd be tossing his cookies."

I nodded, remembering how my usually tough brother turned pale as sand when out in high waves. "He spent the whole time on the ferry to Isle Royale with a barf bag in his hand."

Ryan laughed. "He called it the 'Barf Barge,' remember?"

I nodded and stepped onto the dock. I also remembered the thrill of sleeping outside with moose and wolves running around.

We'd gone on the Isle Royale trip last June. Before a man fell asleep at the wheel and hit Mom's car head on. Before I stole out of the house, sobbing, and faced the nightmare head on. Before I had to try to erase what I'd seen and keep the dark secret.

The secret I'd kept from everyone threatened to surface, but I didn't want to think about what I'd seen. A voice two boats away made me suck in my breath.

Ryan looked at me. "What?" He followed my gaze to where a dark-haired girl on one of the boats waved. Mirra. Another girl popped up from the seat next to her. Brittany.

Mirra waved more frantically. "Hey, you two. We were hoping people would be around."

Knowing Brittany and Mirra, they were hoping older guys, staying in some of the summer vacation homes, would be walking around.

Mirra brushed her long hair away from her eyes and smiled. She'd had it dyed in what a classmate had called a BIV, blue, indigo, violet. It had streaks of blue by the roots blending to an indigo and violet near the ends. "Hi, Ryan. Remember me?"

Ryan cocked his head and flashed his dimples in a grin. I had only one dimple, but even if I had two, I could never pull off the same look. "No, I can't believe it, but I don't."

Mirra stuck out her bottom lip in a fake pout. "Annie and her family took me along to Picnic Island last summer. You boogie-boarded with her brothers. You can really, uh, boogie."

"Picnic Island ... Now I remember. Didn't you find some money in the sand?"

Mirra laughed. "Uh-huh. You helped me dig around for more."

Joey and I helped too, I thought, swallowing hard.

We had reached the boat. "Joey thought for sure we'd found pirate treasure." Mirra giggled.

Ryan pointed to the boat's name. "*Buried Treasures*," he said. "Good name."

Mirra waved her arm. "Come aboard."

Ryan stepped down off the dock, then offered his hand to help me.

My survival instincts kicked in. When I didn't move, Ryan gave me a questioning look. How could I communicate to him that Mirra had been ignoring me for the past six months? That I'd overheard Mirra and Brittany talking about me the night they didn't realize I was in the bathroom stall. That if I joined them now, I'd set myself up to be hurt again.

He dropped his voice. "Don't leave me all alone with them." When his teasing smile didn't win me over, he added, "Come on. Join the party."

Party. It was that word, bringing up the memory of the hair clip and the hope to be a normal girl again, that drew me. I took a step, then another until I was onboard.

Brittany held up two soda cans. "Thirsty?" She didn't have Mirra's gorgeous golden brown skin tone or large brown eyes, but she and Mirra had matching bodies, size four with curves. Brittany's tight orange tank top reflected the setting sun, spotlighting the friend-thief with every last ray.

"Yeah," Ryan said. "I'll take one."

Brittany handed him one, then extended the other to me. "It's diet."

I felt her eyes on my body, a body several sizes larger than hers and Mirra's. I muttered, "No thanks."

Mirra might have caught my tone because she turned on the charm. "It's great to see you, Annie."

I raised my eyebrows in reply and she had the decency to look embarrassed. Other than coming to Mom's funeral and saying the meaningless *I'm so sorry*, and *I can't believe she's gone*, Mirra had ignored me for months.

Ryan gave the boat the once-over. I'd ridden in *Buried Treasures* many times. It was smaller than most of the boats docked in Friendly, Maine, and its tan canopy roof was showing its age, but Ryan was focused on the motor.

Mirra and Brittany followed him. "Mom and I are trying to convince Dad to get a new boat," Mirra said, "the kind that has glitter in the paint."

Ryan turned to me, widening his eyes in an is-she -really-this-stupid question.

"Dad taught me how to drive it," Mirra said. She seemed to wait for Ryan to show he was impressed, but he was squatting to study the motor.

"So, Ryan," Brittany asked, "will you be here all summer?"

He straightened up. "Uh-huh. Annie's dad is letting me crash with them. I got a job at the marina."

"Let's sit." Brittany pointed to the seat across from her, leaving Mirra's and my seats the farthest away.

"What do you do there?" Mirra quickly asked.

"I'm a guide." His eyes shifted from Mirra back to Brittany.

"What a fun job," she said. "I like to fish."

Brittany liked to fish? Right. If Mirra and I were still friends, I'd have looked her way so we could roll our eyes.

Mirra had moved the yellow inflatable emergency lifeboat so we had more room. We both sat while Ryan talked about how he hoped the warm weather would bring in tourists.

"So, where does your family live?" Brittany asked.

"A small town a hundred miles west of here. I could've taken a job at a hamburger place at home, but I'd much rather fish."

Brittany lowered her voice. "I bet you'll make great tips."

Like me, Ryan was cursed with the Bardo fair skin, and he turned to hide his blush. "So," he said, glancing at the line of moored boats, "I'm going to take a quick look at the boats before it gets any darker. Then we'd better get back. We're watching Beetle-eater with Steven."

I'd forgotten we'd told my brother we'd join him at 8:00 for another episode with the survivalist.

"Mind if we walk with you?" Brittany asked.

"Nope." Ryan climbed out first and extended his hand. Brittany took it, her glitzy sandals clicking on the wooden pier. As he held his hand out to me, Brittany gave me a second narrow-eyed once-over. Was she taking in my unpainted toenails that had never seen a pedicure? My no-name jeans or my shapeless sea turtle T-shirt? Probably all three.

I was the one blushing now. "I ... I'll see you at the house, Ryan." Ryan threw me a surprised glance but let the girls lead him away.

"You probably didn't recognize me because of my new hair," Mirra was telling Ryan.

Shells cut into my bare feet, but I was so confused I hardly noticed. What had happened? Did Mirra's talking to me mean she wanted to be friends again? And if she did, could I forgive her?

I climbed the rocky hill toward the road. Mirra's house stood apart from the others, its huge deck already decorated with pots of colorful flowers. When our cottage came into view, its empty window boxes shouted at me. Yesterday, I'd thought it was too early in the season to set plants outside. Tonight, though, I made a plan to pick up the coral-colored impatiens Mom had always liked.

The porch door creaked as I entered the kitchen and walked into the living room. My brothers sat on opposite ends of the couch. Steven stared intently at the TV. His hair needed washing and he had a streak of grease on his cheek.

"Where's Ryan?" he asked, his gaze shifting for only a second.

"He'll be here in a minute. He's checking out the, uh, boats." Steven had started to notice girls, and his lifted eyebrows let me know he wasn't fooled.

Ever since Steven got in trouble at school, Dad made sure to spend more time with him. Unlike Joey, Steven never talked about missing Mom. Not long ago, though, I'd seen him sobbing quietly, gripping the marshmallow roasting stick he had whittled for Mom last summer. When he heard me approaching, he took off down the beach, the stick still clutched in his hand.

I sat down and Joey snuggled up next to me. He'd be turning nine this summer, and I knew that soon he'd be embarrassed to cuddle like this.

The boys, intent on the end of a cop show, looked up several minutes later when the screen door banged closed. I tried to read Ryan's expression. Had he made plans with Brittany?

Dad stepped inside, took off the boots he always wore, and sat at the dining room table. "It's just starting," I called to him.

"Oh, good." I saw him slyly flipping through the mail, though. I know he wanted—and needed—to pay bills.

I happily settled in to watch scenes of fire building, gutting animals, building a shelter, and basic survival activities. All of which were less confusing than trying to figure out Mirra.

After watching Beetle-eater gut a rabbit, I turned to Steven. "Watching that made me want to shower, but you can go first."

"Nah. It's vacation. I don't have to worry about showering."

Oh, great. How would Mom have handled this? I looked to Dad, but he was bent over a calculator.

I locked the bathroom door and caught my reflection in the mirror. I told myself not to compare my body with Mirra and Brittany's, but I knew boys would. I resembled my dad's side of the family. His sisters were big and shapeless, without noticeable waists. I'd tried doing twisting waist exercises every night but gave up since I never noticed a difference.

The warm shower made me feel better. After slipping into my robe, I monitored Joey's teeth brushing, then sat on his bed. He grabbed *Where the Red Fern Grows* from his desk. We were nearing the end.

"I can't wait for tomorrow," Joey said. "If Dad says yes, can we go shopping for puppy things?"

"We'll see."

Joey settled in to listen to me read, his glazed eyes telling me he had already transformed himself into Billy, romping off with his hounds.

* * *

The next morning, I dressed, then pulled out the frying pan and griddle. Ryan, who had to sleep on the couch since we didn't have an extra bed, shuffled toward the bathroom. "Morning," he mumbled.

"Morning," I answered quickly, turning the bacon down. I'd burned it again.

Dad walked in. "Thanks for making breakfast, honey."

"Bacon's burned and pancakes look gummy," I said.

Ryan, Steven, and Joey came in and filled their plates. Dad patted Steven's back and tousled Joey's shaggy head before starting coffee.

"How about trying that new go-kart place this morning?"

"Cool!" Steven said.

"What time do you work again, Ryan?"

"I have training at 6:00 tonight."

Dad kissed my forehead. "You'll come along, won't you, Annie?"

"Thanks, but I'd like to stay here, maybe text Hailey and see her one last time. She's leaving the day after tomorrow to stay with her dad."

Dad looked at me. He knew I'd stopped hanging around with Mirra, but we'd never talked about it. "Maybe you want to spend some time today looking at the city's summer flyer. They might have tennis lessons."

"No," I answered quickly. Mirra and I had taken tennis lessons together last summer. Everything had been fine then. Six months later, though, she'd started snubbing me.

In January, I overheard Mirra tell Brittany about my embarrassing dressing room nightmare. In February, I'd stood in the bathroom stall, my hand covering my mouth to keep the sobs from bursting out. A few weeks later, Mom was killed. Mirra had come to her funeral, but she'd stood stiffly and her words to me had felt false. When she looked like she was going to hug me, I had stepped away.

"How about joining the swim team?" When Dad's forehead wrinkled like that, I knew he was worried. I'd overheard him talking to Grandma on the phone recently. *She used to be running from morning 'til night with Mirra. Now she's always alone ... trying so hard to fill her mother's shoes ... much too serious ... needs to be a kid and have fun. If only Dawn were here.*

Yes, if only Mom were here. Dad's shirt collar was raised on one side. If Mom were here, she would straighten it for him.

"I have enough to do this summer," I said. "Hailey's mom asked me if I'd be her guinea pig. She's putting together an online course on how to make YouTube videos and needs me to act in some."

Dad looked uncertain. "Be careful with what you put on the internet."

"I know, Dad. So, anyway, that'll keep me busy. And I," I paused long enough that my voice wouldn't break, "also wondered about spending time at Grandma and Grandpa's, working with the horses." Mom and I had often ridden together at their farm, and I needed to ride more than ever.

"Sure, we can make that happen."

I nodded. Joey cleared his throat. "Oh, and Joey and I have something to ask you about later."

"Okay."

Joey gave me a thank-you look filled with hope.

After breakfast, Dad and the boys trooped out of the kitchen. "We'll be back in an hour or two," Dad said, waving.

"Have fun." I felt a strange twinge as the car pulled away.

I grabbed my phone to call Hailey and discovered it was dead. I was about to charge it when the neighbor's dog gave his warning bark. I looked out the window and braced myself.

Seeing Mirra heading to my house was like ripping the scab off an unhealed cut.

She'd French-braided her hair and had somehow made her eyes look even more enormous. She wore tight jeans, a shirt that brought out the colors in her dyed hair, and carried a bag along with something hot pink. Her jacket, I realized. I'd seen Brittany wear a matching one. Mirra and I had once had matching jackets. Those days were long gone.

She rang the doorbell. Should I pretend that I wasn't home? If I stayed inside, she'd never know. Just like she'd never known that I was in the bathroom stall the night of the basketball game.

"God," Brittany had said, "did you see what Annie Bardo's wearing? Something she got at a garage sale, I bet."

Mirra had snickered and gone on to tell Brittany the most embarrassing thing that had ever happened to me. She'd been with me when I tried on a bodysuit guaranteed to slim me down a size. I had to pull and yank to get it on, then couldn't get out of the darn thing. I had to ask Mirra to call the clerk in for help. She ended up needing to cut me out of it! Brittany had squealed and snorted hearing the story.

Mirra rang the bell again. Why had she stopped over instead of calling or texting? I still had the same number. Maybe seeing me yesterday made her want to apologize in person. My heart skipped, and I held my breath. If I let her walk away, I'd never find out.

I took a step toward the door, grabbed the handle, held my breath, and opened it.

Mirra pivoted back. "Oh." She raised her over-plucked eyebrows. "You *are* home."

"Yeah, I was, um, ... in the bathroom."

Mirra stepped into the kitchen. She looked past me. "I wanted to see if you and Ryan could go to

Picnic Island today. Brittany and some other kids will be there."

Ryan. Maybe he'd pair up with Brittany, and Mirra and I could hang out together.

"We thought we'd have a beginning-of-the-summer party. Brittany's boat is too full so we should go separate. I'm supposed to help set up."

"Ryan's go-karting." I glanced at the kitchen clock. "He'll be back in an hour or so."

"Oh." Mirra's shoulders drooped. "Maybe we could leave a note. Would your dad let Ryan take your boat out?"

"Probably."

"Or if not, maybe your dad could drop him off out there and we'd bring him back."

I hesitated a moment longer, hoping this wasn't just about Ryan. Should I change my mind? Then I remembered Joey's comment about wanting a puppy so he didn't have to go through the whole summer without something special. I didn't want to be alone, either. Might as well take a chance. "Yeah, okay," I said. I grabbed a pencil and paper and scribbled a note.

After setting it on the table, I snatched a bag of chips from the cupboard to contribute to the picnic. I grabbed the wide-brimmed raffia sunhat Hailey had given me. My windbreaker was in the wash, so I scurried to the hall closet and grabbed the coral fleece that used to belong to Mom. Since she often wore it when she rode at Grandma and Grandpa's, it still had a slight horsey smell, which I intended never to wash out.

I headed to my bedroom to find my phone, but remembered it wasn't charged. I left it. Mirra always carried her phone, so no big deal if I didn't take mine. I saw the hair clip on the dresser and felt a strong urge to grab it. I swept my hair up and clipped it.

Gulls called as I followed Mirra out the door.

CHAPTER TWO
MAYDAY! MAYDAY!

The salty air seemed especially heavy as Mirra and I headed toward *Buried Treasures*. Slashes of orange and red from the sunrise still remained in the sky. *Red sky at night; sailor's delight. Red sky in the morning, sailors take warning.* I might have paused to study the sky, but I spotted two older fishermen, bait buckets in hand, ambling down the weather-beaten pier. One was bent over his phone. Gulls squawked over their heads, hoping for castoff minnows and giving Mirra an opening to break our awkward silence. "Seagulls sure are noisy."

I wanted to correct her, let her know there wasn't such a thing as a seagull, that these seabirds were herring gulls, but I resisted. Mirra had accused me more than once of acting like a know-it-all, calling me Professor Bardo.

The gulls, giving up on the fishermen, picked away on shore. Mom used to say people should pay closer attention to the actions of birds. If they're acting especially hungry, watch for bad weather.

"So," Mirra said casually, "doesn't it feel great to be out of middle school?"

Before I could answer, her phone signaled a text. She bent over reading it. I noticed she'd upgraded her phone. I was lucky to have one at all, and probably would need to keep the one I had until I got a full-time job.

Mirra sent the text. Had she contacted her dad, telling him we were ready to go? Or had she answered another question from her new best friend.

Buried Treasures rocked gently in the waves. Mirra stepped aboard. I followed and stood next to her under the canopy roof. After pulling two apples out of the bag Mirra carried, she stuck them in her jacket pockets. It looked like Mirra's picnic contribution was paper plates, napkins, plastic silverware, apples, candy bars, and granola bars. She took my chips and tucked the big bag under the boat's bow.

Although it was cloudy and she was under a canopy, she whipped on a pair of sunglasses that had been on the dash. She turned to me like she expected something. If she was waiting for me to tell her she looked cool, she'd better not hold her breath.

The raffia hat Hailey had decorated for me included a band of fabric with horses galloping along the ocean's shore and sea birds following behind. I put it on and tightened the strap so it would stay on even in the wind.

Mirra moved a blue cooler to the middle so she could open the canopy's side windows to let in the breeze. I sat on my hands so I wouldn't follow behind her, snapping them in place like they should be.

Once at the wheel, Mirra pulled a key out of her pocket and a piece of paper from under the seat. "My cheat sheet," she explained. Glancing at the list, she flipped on various switches and started the motor. "Half a tank of gas should be enough."

"When's your dad coming?" I scanned the beach.

"He's working. I'm taking us out."

As Mirra slipped into her jacket, I thought back and realized she'd never said her father was taking us. I'd assumed it. I looked toward Mirra's house as if I could conjure up Mr. Peck but, when he didn't appear, I whipped my head back to study her. "I don't know about this. Your dad lets you take this out alone?"

"He says I can as long as I'm with someone else."

I was pretty sure her dad had meant an adult, not another fourteen-year-old. I was about to ask if she'd taken the boater safety course and, if she hadn't, I would tell her I didn't want to go, when she started the motor without a problem. She used her free hand to pass me an orange life jacket and grabbed another one for herself. She buckled it while driving. Maybe she truly knew what she was doing. She steered past the pier.

Mirra was so short she had to stand on tiptoes to see over the bow. She studied the GPS and sped up. "I have Picnic Island programmed in."

I caught sight of the two fishermen walking back on the pier. "Uh, Mirra, those guys must have decided not to go out. Did you check the weather?"

"We're just going a little ways." She steered with one hand and tugged at her tight top with the other. Finally, she took off her sunglasses, the better to show off her clear skin and huge brown eyes. Yes, she was gorgeous. *Mirra, Mirra, on the wall. Who's the fairest of them all?* This queen didn't have to ask. She knew the answer.

To be fair, though, it wasn't just Mirra's looks that made kids want to eat lunch with her or be her lab partner. Her group always had the most fun. My heart ached, remembering.

The wind picked up, blowing the ominous clouds our way. When the steeple of the Catholic church was barely visible anymore, the sky took on a tinge of dark green. I gripped the side of the boat, searching for Picnic Island. That blurry shadow on the horizon might be it. "Are we almost there? I don't like the look of those clouds."

Mirra zipped up her jacket. "We're only like ten minutes away. I was hoping we'd have a chance to talk before everyone else comes."

Talk, as in apologize? Why now, after half a year? I looked at her.

Mirra hesitated and then shouted over the engine's roar and the rising wind. "Remember last summer when your dad brought us to Picnic Island, and I tried to teach your mom and brothers the hula?"

So, this "talk" wouldn't start with an apology. "Uh-huh," I said, because I did remember that fun day. I wrapped my arms around myself. If only I didn't also remember Mirra and Brittany's mean laughter, snickers, and snorts about my being stuck in a bodysuit. After a long silence, I glanced at Mirra. She was stalling.

The sky was turning greener by the minute and the air was as humid as an over-watered greenhouse. "Did you check the weather?" I repeated. When Mirra didn't answer, I knew she hadn't. "Did you even ask to use the boat?"

Mirra shrugged. "Last time Dad and I went out, I drove the whole time, and I even docked it. He said I did great."

No permission, and no forecast. And didn't kids have to pass a boating test to drive without an adult? I searched and thought I spotted Picnic Island just ahead. We'd throw out the anchor, climb in the rubber raft, and row to the island.

Mirra's metallic black fingernails drummed against the dash. "Oh," Mirra said, as if suddenly remembering. "I wanted to ask you something." She gave me a sideways glance as swells slapped against the boat. "Does Ryan have a girlfriend? Did he say anything about me or Brittany?"

My cheeks stung like someone had slapped them. How could I have been so stupid? To have hoped she'd invited me along as a friend. To have thought she wanted to apologize. She only wanted to find out about Ryan. I ought to tell her how Ryan had rolled his eyes after her stupid comment about wanting a new boat, one that had glitter in the paint. "This has been fun, Mirra," I said, willing my voice not to quaver, "but take me back home." The words had barely left my mouth when thunder cracked in the distance. My skin prickled as I stared at the darkening sky. The wind gusted stronger than before.

"Crap!" Mirra looked toward the horizon. "We better head to the island."

"Yeah, okay. We can wait there until the storm passes."

Red sky at night; sailor's delight. Red sky in the morning, sailors take warning.

Panic made me forget my anger for the moment. I searched for other boaters in case we needed help. None. I tried closing the side windows. But before I could zip the first one, the wind whipped at the canvas and we hit a deep swell. *Buried Treasures* swooped down into it, taking my stomach with it. Water sloshed on the floor. The boat rose high, then slammed into the gray waves again.

Thunder boomed, and I lunged closer to Mirra at the control panel.

"I don't see the island anymore," Mirra said in a high-pitched voice. Water spilled in over one side. She turned the wheel sharply.

"Mirra!" I screamed.

"I'm supposed to steer into the waves," she mumbled. She turned the wheel again.

"How do we get this water out?"

"Uh, yeah, there's a button. Some kind of pump." Before she found it, though, a wind blast ripped the boat's canopy half off. Mirra cut the speed. The canvas flapped like a distress flag, then split off and blew away. The boat spun. Another huge swell appeared at the bow.

The whimpers coming from Mirra added to my terror.

"Give me your phone," I shouted.

She clutched the wheel with one hand and pulled out her phone with the other. I clung onto the dash and hit 9 1 before a gigantic tower of greenish-gray water blasted over us. It soaked the phone. I caught my breath and tried punching the final 1. Please, oh, please. But nothing. A wall of water crashed onto the boat, soaking it more. Icy water sloshed around our ankles. The bow tilted to sea level again. "Hang on—" When I grabbed for the side-rail, the phone dropped to my feet. There was no chance of grabbing it—I was holding on for dear life as wave after wave washed onto the deck. The boat's motor died. The storm was sweeping us out of the bay and into the open sea.

"Call the Coast Guard!" I screamed, remembering the radio.

Mirra pressed a button and shouted, "Coast Guard! Coast Guard!"

Nothing except static.

"Mayday! Mayday!" Mirra shrieked.

The bow tilted up, and the cooler slid, hitting the stern and sounding like a gunshot. Clutching onto the handrail, I held my breath. A saltwater wall, taller than any before, swept over us. Coughing and sputtering, I looked for Mirra. She was gripping the wheel. A scream stuck in my throat as the boat plunged.

When the wave sliced over us, it washed my legs out from under me. I closed my eyes as the freezing cold ocean ripped away my hat and poured down on me.

The boat pitched sideways. I lost my grip and tumbled into the raging water.

CHAPTER THREE
CASTAWAYS

cy water. Life jacket barely keeping me above it. A strange gurgling sound. The boat.

Sinking.

Something tangled around my ankle. Pulling me under. The ski rope!

I clawed at it to unhook it. The life jacket tried to keep me up, but the sinking boat fought back. Underwater. Grasping for the rope. Dragging me deeper by the second.

My fingers touched metal. I pinched the clip. Come on ... come on ... open ...

Free!

Air! Gulping, coughing, spitting. More gurgling noises from the boat. Sinking fast.

A faint cry. "Help!"

I tried to see past the waves, towering overhead, then dropping away. "Mirra!" The ocean's roar swallowed up my words. "Where are you?"

"Help—"

A wave cut off her cry. "Mirra?" Every time a wave lifted me, I searched. Only a spot of yellow. The emergency life raft! Mirra had a life jacket. Better grab the raft first. I kicked and propelled toward it, still searching the valley of the waves. "Mirra?" I screamed again.

Gigantic waves. Another blast of saltwater stung my eyes.

"Annie!"

"I'm coming! Getting the life raft first!" A wave helped me grab it. I pulled where it said "Pull" and with a poof, it inflated. A two-person circular raft.

Kicking and pulling for all I was worth, I dragged myself over the side, into the raft's covered bottom. I searched for Mirra's life jacket. There, a spot of orange. "Paddle for the raft!"

Mirra had never learned to swim and her arms just beat against the water. She seemed to spin in circles. I'd need to go to her.

I tried paddling with my arm, but it was only luck that the raft floated within inches of Mirra. "Grab on!"

Mirra's fingers clenched a handhold. A mountainous wave sent us high then low, ripping her hand from the raft. "AH!" she screamed.

I tried to steer the raft toward her, but the waves were sending me in the opposite direction. "Swim!"

Mirra splashed wildly, but she didn't get any closer. Soon the waves would take her away.

Then, a miracle. A swell swept the raft to within feet of her. No time to lose.

"Grab on!"

Mirra's hands reached and caught the raft.

"I'll pull you in! Kick!" I grabbed her lifejacket and tugged. "Kick harder!" She slid on top, and I dragged her inside seconds before I saw another monstrous wave closing in. "Hold on tight!" We both grasped the life raft's handholds as the swell lifted us up and slammed us back down.

The waves threw us high before plunging us back. "Please don't tip over," I whispered.

My eyes stung, but I wasn't about to risk letting go of the boat to wipe them. Thunder boomed, rain poured down, waves swelled, and the wind roared. I tried to shut it all out, but Mirra's screams pierced through all of it like a sharp blade.

The storm raged on. All I could do was shiver and hang on. I ignored the numbness from my fingers to my toes. Nothing, NOTHING, would make me let go.

* * *

The life raft rose and fell, rose and fell. Even though the rain had stopped, gray swells kept coming. We must have been in the raft an hour or more, and we were probably miles from shore. Mirra sat sniffling as we drifted further and further from home.

Cold. So cold.

Mirra patted her jacket pocket. "If only we had a phone."

"Your dad's at work?" I asked through chattering teeth.

"Uh huh. Mom had exercise class this morning. She should be home by now, though."

"Did you leave a note?"

"No, I was going to call her."

I shot her a look. "So they don't even know the boat's gone?"

She shook her head. "D-do you think Brittany and the others are on Picnic Island?" Mirra had wrapped her arms around her body trying to get warm. "If we were close enough, th-they might have seen us t-tip over. C-could have called for help."

"Maybe. The call you got. Earlier. Was it from Brittany?"

"No, N-Natalie. Saying she couldn't make it."

"I don't think anyone came. They probably saw the forecast and stayed put." Sitting in icy water didn't cool down my anger, and I didn't regret sounding so snotty.

My eyes constantly searched the empty horizon. A spot of blue drew my eyes. It was only the cooler, but when it bobbed close enough, I grabbed it. The raft had a loop of black cord that I slipped through the handle to tie it in place. I lifted the lid: shirts, shorts, and pants that must belong to Mirra's parents, a baseball cap, box of matches, four green cups, a sheathed knife, one granola bar, two bottles of water, and a large tin that once held cookies.

Mirra, who hadn't budged an inch to help, suddenly brightened. "Look inside that container. Dad said he put some safety stuff in a cookie tin." She leaned closer.

I popped off the lid. "A flare gun and cartridges! No, only one cartridge."

"So if we see a boat, we can shoot it off!"

"Right!" I looked around hopefully but saw only waves.

"I'm taking a water." Mirra unscrewed the top. "Have to rinse out my mouth."

Only two waters. "We'd better be careful," I said, taking one. "This is all we have."

"Dad talked about needing to restock. We have these too." She pulled two apples out of her jacket pockets and added them to the cooler. She swished water in her mouth, then spit it into the rolling waves. My mouth watered as she took a drink. I'd love to rinse out my mouth too, but I only took a sip, letting it drizzle down my throat. I forced myself to put the bottle back in the cooler.

Mirra and I both sat cross-legged. Hours passed as we rode the waves and swiveled our heads hoping to spot another boat. Finally, Mirra pulled out the granola bar.

"You'll save it for later, right?" I asked. "We might get even hungrier."

Mirra studied the granola bar a moment, then returned it to the cooler. A long time passed in silence as we watched for rescuers. Mirra stared at me, glassy-eyed. "Do you think our parents have any idea where we are?"

I pictured my dad, Steven, and Joey leaving the go-kart track. They might drive by Dad's work to check on things. Dad had the day off, but he'd probably stop by the nature center and make sure Tom, the other educator, wasn't too swamped. He'd look to see what groups were coming in and make sure the summer intern had fed Merlin, the rehabilitated great horned owl used for education. I usually enjoyed spending as much time there as he wanted. So did Joey. I could only hope Steven was as impatient as usual and nagged Dad to get going.

Once he got home, he'd read my note and study the sky. He'd try my phone and find that I hadn't brought it. He'd call Mirra's house or run over. They'd check and see that *Buried Treasures* was still out. How long would it take for them to call the Coast Guard?

I'm sorry to have to tell you this, a voice might be saying right now. But there's no trace of them.

Mirra sat up straighter. "Annie! The Coast Guard probably has sonar detectors, you know, like fish locators. Maybe they can use them to find where the boat sank and track us."

I wanted to believe it, but we hadn't seen any helicopters or signs of a rescue team. I guessed it was supper time, and darkness was only hours away.

"Maybe parts of the boat, like the canvas top will float in," Mirra continued, "and they can study their maps on currents and figure out where we've drifted. Do you think they'll find us soon?"

Find this tiny raft in the vast sea? Hardly any chance of that, especially after a storm that had blown us who knows where. Should I share my thoughts? No, it seemed too cruel, so I only said, "I hope so."

Hope. We still had hope.

* * *

While the raft rocked, Mirra and I kept watch. *Please come, someone. Help us.*

When darkness fell, so did the temperature. I couldn't stop shivering. "How about we share the extra clothes?" I asked Mirra.

We split up her parents' clothes. I helped steady the raft as Mirra changed. "This is tricky," she said, trying to peel off her tight jeans.

I thought of my dressing room nightmare. As I struggled to shed my own wet jeans, I looked toward the sea. I'd choose trying to shimmy out of a tight bodysuit any day over facing this cold dark nothingness.

The dry pants soon became wet from the bottom of the raft and I continued shivering. To make things worse, I desperately needed to pee. I should have taken care of that when I was half dressed. Maybe I could wait a little longer.

Mirra was either sleeping or pretending to. I tried to relax while sitting up, but the lifejacket made resting my head and neck impossible. I thought about taking it off, but if I fell asleep and we hit a wave, I could roll off. Besides, someone should stay alert in case of a helicopter or a search and rescue boat.

The night blackened and clouds blocked any stars or the moon. It was the darkest dark I'd ever seen. Camping in the wilderness, my family always had a fire or at least flashlights. Here, there was no light at all.

I pulled on my ear, a nervous habit I'd picked up from Dad. I'd first seen him do it the day Grandma and he picked me up early from school and told me there'd been a terrible accident. My world changed that day ...

The need to use the bathroom was now desperate. Do I slip into the freezing, rolling waves that could be full of sharks? No, I wouldn't chance it.

First I pulled out the cookie tin. The pants Mirra'd given me were big, but still, getting them off was a struggle and the extra bobbing made Mirra ask, "What's going on?"

"Going to the bathroom." I squatted over the tin.

At the pinging sound, Mirra groaned. "Pass that over here when you're done." A few minutes later she grumbled, "Peeing in a tin. Ugh." After she pulled up her mom's jeans, she emptied the tin, rinsed it and set it back in the cooler. "This is too much."

It was her snobby tone that made me lose it. "Too much is taking a boat out without knowing how to drive it. Too much is going without checking the forecast." I lay down on the life raft's floor, using my bent arm as a pillow. "I'm resting. You're on watch." I closed my eyes.

My mind drifted back to this morning when I'd watched the gulls begging for treats from the fishermen. I tried to recall seeing gulls while we cruised toward Picnic Island, but I couldn't remember a single bird. Now I realized why. They'd all flown off to safety.

Chapter Four
"Is Anyone There?"

The ocean was calm enough that I didn't have to grip the raft. Seeing nothing but ocean and sky, I hadn't a clue where we were.

Mirra was on watch so I could sleep, but I kept thinking of green water, thrashing arms, my leg trapped in a tangle of rope, dragging me deeper and deeper.

"Annie?"

I sat up. The clouds had cleared allowing a few stars to shine. I must have slept an hour or two.

"I need to lie down," Mirra said. "Sleep."

"Okay." The hollowness in her voice scared me. "I'll watch."

I peered into the endless swells for what could have been an hour. *Splash!* "Hello?" I yelled.

Mirra jerked upright. "Have they come?"

Silence. "Sorry, it was probably just a fish."

The raft rocked. Mirra whispered. "I wonder what our parents are doing now?"

My one remaining parent was probably pacing and digging his fingers down to the roots of his hair. He and Mirra's parents would be on the phone with the police, Coast Guard, or friends with boats.

Mirra groaned. "My mom gave up smoking six months ago. Last weekend we went out to celebrate. This'll probably put her over the edge and she'll start again." She licked her lips and spoke just above a whisper. "It's not going to do their rocky marriage any good, either."

Her parents were having trouble? I had no idea.

"I need some water." Mirra uncapped her bottle. It was down to half, but mine was nearly full. As she drank, I thought back to our Easter egg hunt in third grade. Mirra ate her entire chocolate bunny right away, but I nibbled at mine. It was mean of me, but I'd made sure Mirra knew I still had chocolate left. Now, as I took a tiny sip, I also wanted Mirra to see I had more so she wouldn't drink unless she had to.

After we capped our bottles, I pointed. "That's the North Star, so this must be west."

Mirra didn't seem to hear. "Anyone there? Help! Anyone?"

Did she think her calling would magically make land or a boat appear? She called again to the empty horizon, this time even more desperately. Finally, she sniffled and curled herself into a soggy ball.

Joey had curled up in my bed the same way the night of Mom's funeral.

Joey ... he was always misplacing things, but he was smart. Mom had called him her 'thinker.' He amazed his Sunday school teacher by asking deep questions like *Why did God create us?* and *Were there dinosaurs on Noah's Ark?* Joey also loved stories and books, especially if they had dogs in them.

Steven ... He wasn't book smart, but when we camped we counted on him to find dry wood, start the fire, and grill his famous burgers. I remembered watching him take seconds on pancakes yesterday morning. Had I really been warm and dry at home less than twenty-four hours ago?

Dad ... He relied on me, especially to help with the boys. Every night now I made sure we'd locked the doors and my brothers were safe in bed. Otherwise, I couldn't fall asleep.

Now I was depending on Dad. As the wind continued to calm, I whispered, "Find me, Dad. Find me."

I searched the gray ocean, but there were only rolling swells. When I felt myself falling asleep, I splashed water on my face. Muscles cramping, I repositioned my body, but everything still hurt.

Mirra groaned and sat up. Her once carefully braided hair was now blowing in her eyes. She massaged her arms and stretched out her legs, knocking them into mine. "Anything?" she asked.

I shook my head.

She patted her stomach. "Hungry. I wish I hadn't been dieting. Brittany and I set a goal to eat under 1,500 calories a day." She choke-laughed. "I'm meeting my goal."

The memory of her telling Brittany about my trying on the bodysuit made my voice sharp. "It's your turn to take over the watch. I did it most of the night."

"Yes, sir!"

"Hey!" I couldn't stop myself. "You got us into this. Taking off without checking the weather, and when you hardly knew anything about driving a boat." Mirra might be cute and a size four, but she was clueless. I lay down, closed my eyes, and went back in time.

Mirra, I knew, hadn't stopped hanging around with me just because I wasn't a size four. We'd been heading for trouble a year ago. She'd rolled her eyes last spring when I'd tried to talk her into getting up at 5:00 a.m. to help volunteers net migrating birds. We'd get to examine them for body fat and band them. She knew how much I loved stuff like that, but she hadn't come with me.

To be perfectly honest, I'd been sighing and clicking my tongue at her more often than I could count, especially at her suggestions we experiment with eye makeup or hang out at the basketball court where the high school guys played on warm nights. I was okay with watching the boys from a distance, but Mirra wanted to get them to notice her and talk to her. "Let's work on our flirting skills," she'd said. The thought of approaching strange guys terrified me.

I was glad Hailey and I were getting to know one another. She was fun in a different way. She had all these projects going—from researching how beluga whales communicate to designing funky hats. She had signed up for three online classes this summer and would have signed up for more if her mom hadn't set a limit.

Mirra's water bottle crinkled, bringing me back to the present. I heard a swish like she took a drink.

I tried to push water from my mind, but what I thought about instead was a pitcher of lemonade... pouring the sweet drink into a tall glass... decorating the glass with a slice of lemon... bringing the wetness to my mouth.

When I woke, the sun was rising. I sat up. Mirra's pained expression let me know there had been no signs of rescuers. I licked my cracked lips. The ocean swells were definitely gentler this morning, and the sky was cloud-free. "Let's try paddling. If Maine is to the west, we should row away from the rising sun. Right?"

Mirra shrugged.

I lay on my stomach and used my left arm to push through the waves. Again and again, I paddled. I thought about telling Mirra she ought to take a turn, but paddling didn't seem to help. I kept quiet.

Mirra swayed from side to side. "I really need something to eat."

Two apples, my mind chanted, *that's all we have.* "Let's share half an apple," I said.

Mirra opened the cooler. I found the knife and cut the crisp apple into quarters. After I handed Mirra a piece, I took one myself. Forcing myself to eat it slowly, I savored every bite.

"Let's have more," Mirra said. "I'm starving."

My stomach agreed, but one of us had to be cautious. "We'd better wait."

"You think you know everything. It was the same when you and the other kids laughed at me in science class."

I stared at her.

"Remember. Mrs. Clark was making us flip a coin to see what traits our baby dragon would have."

"Yeah, for our genetics unit."

"And without thinking, I said something dumb."

I was trying to remember details when Mirra, like a hungry fish going for a shiny lure, grabbed another chunk of apple and stuffed it in her mouth.

"Stop!" I yelled. "We have to make it last!"

Mirra chewed quickly. "You aren't in charge. I brought these. They're mine!" She snagged the second apple, waved it in the air, and took a huge bite from it too.

"No!" I lunged. I hit her hand, and the apple fell into the sea. Both of us grabbed for it, but it bobbed out of our reach. We tried paddling toward it, but it disappeared in the water. I thought about jumping in for it, but the icy water and the fear of sharks stopped me.

"Now you did it!" Mirra barked.

"Me? If you weren't such a spoiled, selfish—" I pressed my lips together.

By midday the clouds had broken up. I finally remembered Mirra's comment about the dragons. After the teacher had given us the assignment, Mirra had looked at her and said, "Wait, you mean dragons are real?'"

I had laughed along with everyone else.

"I think this waiting is making us crazy," I finally said, hoping she knew it was an apology.

Mirra nodded, and her gaze softened. "We've lost most of the clouds. We're going to get burned." She dug out her dad's cap, started to put it on, then passed it over to me. "You can wear it first."

I pulled it low to cover my face. "Thanks."

My T-shirt and borrowed pants were dry, but I wished I could get the salty film off my skin. I closed my eyes against the sun's glare. Dancing flashes of light beat in my brain, giving me a headache.

When I opened them and a boat-shaped object appeared in the distance, I shot to attention. "Mirra, look!" I pointed. "Is it coming this way?"

Mirra shaded her eyes. "No, I think it's going away! The flare!" She dug through the cooler. "I'll shoot it off. Dad showed me how."

I gave her room, keeping my eye on the disappearing boat. "Hurry!"

Mirra grabbed the cartridge from the cooler and popped it in the red pistol-like gun. She was about to raise it when *Click! Boom!* It fired the flare straight down into the ocean!

"No!" I screamed as it sizzled to nothing.

Mirra groaned. "I ... I hardly touched the trigger."

Frantically, we waved our hands and yelled, but the boat kept going.

Why had I trusted her? I should have taken over! I couldn't look at Mirra.

The flare's burning smell blew away, and the other boat became a speck. When I met Mirra's eyes, I nearly snarled. She shot me back a look equally fierce. Fine. I crossed my arms over my chest.

Nausea, as much from the anger and disappointment I felt as the rolling waves, made me wonder if I'd have to throw up over the side. I closed my eyes, but then all I saw was an inventory of our few supplies including a flare gun with no cartridges.

A half hour later, my stomach still felt queasy. It helped to lower my head, close my eyes, and picture myself at home with my family. I was imagining sitting down to dinner with them when the *chop-chop* noise of a helicopter made me open my eyes and jerk my head back. "Helicopter!" Mirra and I screamed at the same time.

I wanted to stand in the raft and wave like a maniac, but I'd tip us over, so instead we waved and screamed, "Here! We're here!" We called until we were hoarse, but the helicopter kept going.

The queasiness overcame me, and I bent over the side. I threw up everything that was in my stomach. Dry heaves took over. When I finally stopped, Mirra patted my hand. "They're still looking for us. They'll be back. The waves make it hard, but it'll get smoother and then they'll be able to see us."

I wiped my mouth. Water. I would just drink a little. I had to force myself not to tilt the bottle up. I would never take water for granted again.

I needed to distract myself. I tucked my long hair up under the cap realizing that it still held the glittery hair clip. I transferred it to my pocket. Was it just yesterday morning that I'd fantasized about wearing my hair up? I was directing all of my energy now to being rescued, not wasting any on thoughts of parties, boyfriends, and hair clips.

Mirra's groan brought me back to reality. "I feel foggy," she said, "like I'm not all here."

She looked dazed and with her messy hair and lips swollen to twice their size, I felt a twinge. "Here," I handed her the cap. "It's your turn."

The sun was sucking all the moisture out of us.

"Thanks. I don't burn like you, but the glare gets to me." I thought of the hat Hailey had designed for me, now floating in the ocean.

Mirra dug in the cooler. "I'll try to make you a hat out of a piece of clothing. I can wet it so it keeps you cooler."

While she fussed with her dad's shirt, I searched for a distraction from the burning sun and thirst. Ryan. I would come right out with it. "So this thing with Ryan. Do you really like him?"

"To tell you the truth," Mirra kept her head down, "it was mostly to see if I could get him to like me over Brittany. Flirt, maybe have a summer fling and be able to tell everyone about it."

You idiot! I wanted to yell. My disgust came out in my tone. "So you took out the boat when you didn't know what you were doing."

"I hadn't planned on taking it out myself. I'd pictured Ryan driving, but after saying I knew how, I was stuck." Mirra fussed some more with the shirt-cap. "I figured I'd impress Ryan if I drove it myself."

Boy worries seemed frivolous now.

Mirra wrapped the shirt around my head turban style, using the arms to tie it in place, and pulled out enough cloth to make a wide brim. I had a flash of a fun summer day when we'd pretended to be models.

"How do I look?" I asked, squinting from the sun.

"Like a model for *Fashion Plate*," she answered.

Fashion Plate! I shot her a look, but she didn't realize I was remembering the store where I'd gotten stuck in the bodysuit. I closed my eyes. How many other kids knew the story? The girls on Mirra's dance team? Did they laugh about it between practicing their routines? Did Hailey know?

After Mirra stopped talking to me, I'd spent more time with Hailey. Hailey loved horses and animals as much as I did. She also enjoyed dressing up old hats with feathers or flowers and selling them at craft fairs. Several women around Friendly had gotten more than one hat. Hailey and her mom also took in foster rabbits and had used long pieces of driftwood to create a fence around their yard. They hid ceramic rabbits and bunnies under bushes or in the grass. On warm days, they let their two pet rabbits out. Joey loved to go over there and search for rabbits—fake and real.

Hailey talked about her rabbits, horses, shopping, boys, and her jewelry-making, but she also talked about needing to do chores. Something I could relate to. And she didn't seem to mind when I'd sometimes stare off into space. Hailey never would have pulled such a stupid stunt as Mirra did, especially not to snag a summer boyfriend.

Mirra shaded her face with her hand. "If only it would cloud up and rain," she mumbled. "We could spread our coats out and get some water; open our mouths and let it all fall in."

I splashed myself with saltwater, wishing for the hundredth time that we could drink it. I dribbled some on my face and arms. "This feels good."

Mirra splashed herself too.

Long minutes passed. From the angle of the sun, I guessed it was three or four o'clock. "We could be close to shipping lanes, but I'm not sure. I think land is this way." I pointed to the left, lay on my stomach and tried paddling with one arm.

"Nuh-uh. It's that way." Mirra pointed the opposite direction.

I ignored her and kept paddling.

"Quit it!" she shouted. "You're going farther out."

"Shut your mouth!" I shot back, glaring at her. "You're the reason we're in this mess. If you didn't want to flirt with Ryan, I'd be home right now."

"I wish you were home too," Mirra snapped, "so I wouldn't have to look at you."

CHAPTER FIVE
BLISTERS AND BOILS

The sun was still intense when the yellow life raft switched directions, drifting farther to the east. I usually felt pretty smart about science and nature, but I knew nothing about ocean currents. I didn't know if they were sweeping us out to the middle of the ocean or toward Greenland.

After our fight, Mirra had closed her eyes and fallen asleep. The back of my neck knotted with tension. Mirra, the queen, got to sleep, leaving me as the only lookout.

When she finally moved, I gave in to my exhaustion. "It's my turn to sleep." I rubbed my forehead, hoping to ease the coming headache. "Don't fall asleep or we could miss a rescue boat."

She glared at me. Yeah, I had talked to her like she was a child, but that's what she deserved.

I didn't totally trust her, but I had to rest. It was hard to find a comfortable position, but I could close my eyes. Purple and yellow sunbursts exploded in my mind's eye. I imagined sunglasses, a shade tree, and a tall glass of ice water. I drifted off.

The sun had dropped to the horizon by the time I woke up. No boat or helicopter in sight. Reaching for my water bottle, I realized it was half-empty. Had I really drunk that much? Or had Mirra taken some? I glared at her. Well, two could play that game.

"You can go to sleep now," I offered sweetly. "I'll watch for a while."

Mirra mumbled something I couldn't hear. But she soon appeared to be asleep. I reached across and shook Mirra's water bottle. She only had about four swallows left. I uncapped her bottle, then looked over at her. No. I capped her bottle and put it back. What was I turning into?

Night fell. I forced myself to stay awake by dribbling sea water on my face and body. I fell asleep around midnight, though, and woke at the first hint of daylight. Day three. Would this be the day we die?

As soon as Mirra awoke, she sat up and searched the ocean and my face for any hope. She slumped back. "How many days, do you think, before the Coast Guard gives up?"

"I don't know, but I'd think they'd use both a helicopter and boat." My right arm felt sore. I carefully pulled up my sleeve, expecting sunburn or bruises from slamming into the side of *Buried Treasures*. I found those and something else. "Ewww!" I gasped at pus-filled boils dotting my arm.

Mirra leaned close, wrinkling her nose. She scratched her belly. Lifting up her shirt, she squealed. "What are they?"

"Boils, I think." I wanted to squeal too. "From the saltwater."

Mirra's eyes widened. "We need fresh water."

No kidding. Feeling pushed to the edge, I tried to distract myself. How did that quote go? Something like, *Water, water everywhere, but not a drop to drink.*

I scanned the sea. My heart jumped clear to my throat. "Look!" I pointed to a light-colored shape on the horizon. "It could be a boat! Let's try paddling toward it." We both lay on our stomachs and one-arm paddled, pulling against the water. Then I saw it spout and groaned. "A whale." The disappointment quickly turned to fear. A whale could flip us over with a flick of its tail.

The shape disappeared. I kept watch, praying it wouldn't come near our raft.

After several minutes passed without seeing it again, Mirra let go of the handhold. "We're so far out we don't even see birds." She pulled the cap out of the cooler. "Here, Annie. You can wear it today. I'll wear the turban—" The raft suddenly lurched sideways. Was it the whale I'd seen earlier? But then, under the water's surface, I saw it: dorsal fin, the body built for speed and strength, the deadly jaws.

"Shark!" Mirra yelled, scooting her body closer to the center of the raft.

He'll flip us over. Bite into the raft. And once we're thrashing around in the water—I clutched onto my handholds.

Mirra cried out as silver-blue flashed a second time, rocking the raft.

This couldn't be happening! I bit my chapped lips so hard I tasted blood. The shark circled us again. I

couldn't stop scenes from shark movies flashing in my head. Sharks torpedoing out of the water, jaws open wide, teeth like hooked white knives. The raft rocked again, this time so violently, the green cup we'd used to bail water washed away.

The dorsal fin circled around us faster now, as if the shark knew it was about to feed. A roar came up from somewhere deep inside me. *You think you can flip us over like we're nothing?* I pulled on the rope, bringing the cooler closer to the raft. *You think you can fall asleep at the wheel and kill my mother?* I grabbed the knife. *You think you can laugh at me behind my back and I'll just forget?* I clutched the knife in my hand. *You think I'll give up?*

"Grab my leg," I commanded Mirra. "Don't let me fall in."

"What are you going to do?" she whimpered. But she took a firm hold of my ankle. I raised my arm. The shark's jaws appeared, but I only looked at its eye.

When I slashed towards the shark's eye, my arm was unbelievably strong and dead-on. I pierced that eye, hearing a popping sound a millisecond before I realized my mistake. The angry shark thrashed its tail so hard it launched the flimsy raft out of the water. The weight of the cooler, still tied on, might have kept us from flipping over. Still, ocean water slurped in.

"Bail!" I called to Mirra.

She cupped her hands and frantically flung water. Still clutching the knife, I searched for the shark. A swirl and ... *Whoosh!* The shark's tail slapped at the raft, sending us spinning again. One more slap, seeming like a desperate last attempt. I held my breath and, Yes! The dorsal fin darted away.

Mirra's gasping breaths and her eyes, wide and swimming with terror, made me realize this wasn't a scene from a movie. This had really happened. My whole body shook. I tried to keep watching in case the shark returned, but I knew I was too shaky to do anything if it did.

As the raft rocked like a baby's cradle, I longed to have my father's strong arms around me. But I didn't have his arms. I only had mine.

CHAPTER SIX
CLOSER

The light had faded, changing the tips of the waves to the color of a shark's silvery body. "You were amazing," Mirra said. She made a choking noise that almost sounded like a laugh. "This'll be an awesome story to share at parties."

Mirra, ever the party girl. I should have agreed, but knowing that we'd never have a chance to tell the story unless we bailed made me hand her one of the remaining green cups. I used the tin, and we got most of the water out of the raft.

"I'm so thirsty." Mirra raised her water bottle. Empty. Did she know how much water I had left?

"What if we drank just a little of the saltwater?" she asked.

I shook my head. "You can't. It'll dehydrate you even more."

Mirra reached out and cupped a handful of ocean water.

"My dad told us a story about a boy who drank saltwater and started seeing things," I blurted. "The boy saw flames and jumped overboard." I shook my head again. "No matter how thirsty I get, I'm not drinking it."

Mirra let the water dribble through her fingers. "If only it would rain." She dipped her hand into the water again.

The sun was close to setting. My dirty, sweaty body stank, and I fought the urge to pick at the painful new pus-filled boils on my neck and arms.

"What do you suppose it's like to die from thirst?" Mirra whispered. "Does a person just go to sleep and never wake up?"

My tongue felt swollen, twice its size, but I said, "Think of something else."

"Like water faucets?" She groaned. "Isn't it awesome how you can turn a knob and get all the water you want? Gallons and gallons of water." Mirra smiled dreamily. "Water to drink, to use for showers, even to pour on the ground."

I pictured our refrigerator's dispenser. Crushed ice and clean water.

I sighed and stared off at the sandy-colored cloud, low on the horizon. It almost looked like a sand dune.

"One of us has to keep watch," I told Mirra. When she didn't answer, I sighed. "I'll go first; you take the early morning shift."

"If only I'd have put the bag of picnic stuff in the cooler."

It took me a second to recall three days ago when she'd taken my chips, added it to her bag of candy and granola bars, and set it under the bow. Who knew that one act could possibly mean the difference between life and death.

Mirra licked her lips. "I'd kill for a Snickers bar."

My stomach rumbled at the idea. Melted chocolate, caramel, and peanuts. If I had one, I'd make it last. I'd lick my fingers and thumb, savoring every last bit of it. Or a juicy apple ... How stupid I'd been not to have kept the last apple piece in my mouth longer, gotten every ounce of wetness out of it before swallowing.

Mirra fingered the buckles on her life jacket. "If I got washed overboard again, I'd panic."

I thought about her not knowing how to swim and said, "I'll stay on watch for a while." I scanned for signs of whales, sharks, or boats.

"Thank you." Mirra closed her eyes.

Mirra's mom had secretly talked to me before swim lessons, asking me to see if I could get Mirra to try harder. I had failed at that, like I'd failed at keeping our friendship. Like I was failing now. And my poor family.

Joey ... He and I had planned to talk to Dad about the puppy. What was Joey doing now? Was he clinging to Dad? Steven would have retreated somewhere, sullen and silent. And Dad ... To lose Mom and then me.

The sun peeked out of a cloud bank, making its last brilliant appearance of the day. The gray horizon changed for a few seconds to orange, coral, and then blue. I remembered my science teacher saying that sunrises and sunsets are best if there's a lot of dust in the atmosphere. And that dust was a mixture of many tiny pieces that travel long distances. *Are you looking at the sunset too?* I asked my father. *I'm still alive, Dad. I'm trying to survive until someone finds us.*

The air had gotten cooler, and I wrapped my arms around myself. After Mom's death, we'd started what we called a hug-huddle. The three of us, and sometimes Steven too, would form a tight circle as if trying to keep the sadness from coming inside. Dad, I realized, could be in a hug-huddle with the boys right now, waiting for news about me and trying to hold it together.

Dad must feel as helpless and lost as I did. I flashed back to last summer's camping trip. It was just dad, my brothers, and me. Steven had gotten lost on our first day on Isle Royale. Dad had panicked, charging through heavy brush and calling. We were so remote, no one else was around to help. Dad, Joey, and I searched for hours, and it was just a fluke thing that I happened to find a boot print in the mud that we guessed belonged to Steven. We followed the trail, catching tracks every once in a while. It was almost dark when we heard Steven calling, his voice hoarse and panicky. "Dad?"

"Steven!" Dad, Joey, and I had yelled as we ran toward him. Steven was all scratched up and bleeding. When we hugged him, he cried. When he finally got a grip on himself, he looked embarrassed. That was the last time I'd seen him cry.

I glanced from the empty ocean to the empty sky. Crying would not help Mirra and me get home. Crying would not provide food or water. Crying would not stop us from dying.

Will death be painful? Or will we just drift off to sleep?

The waves sloshed over the raft in a rhythm sounding like a heartbeat. *Lub-dub, Lub-dub, Lub-dub.* When death comes, my heart will stop and this little raft will be my grave until the ocean washes me overboard. Dad and my brothers will never find me. They will never know what happened.

A cloud must have moved, revealing the moon. Its crescent shape reminded me of an inviting finger, one that could be either helpful or ominous. *Come to me*, it seemed to say. *Closer. Closer. Closer.*

CHAPTER SEVEN
DAY FOUR

For a moment, I didn't remember we were lost at sea. But my aching body, red skin, and sunburned face quickly brought it all rushing back. I sat up and massaged my legs. Mirra and I had both fallen asleep. She looked so still, I called her name. Her whimpers let me know she was still alive.

The fog thinned out. The ghostly picture of a horse appeared on the horizon. I blinked, and the image vanished.

I was hallucinating. Was I dying? Maybe my horse-loving Mom had sent one to escort me to heaven.

Sun broke out from beneath the clouds, and I thought I saw a spot of land and heard gulls. I closed my eyes to listen better. I was hearing birds. Gulls.

The fog lifted, and the water appeared lighter in color. I smelled the air. Something was different—a fresh scent. A chill traveled up my spine. "Mirra! Wake up!" A long, sandy-colored shape! "Mirra! Land! I think I see a shoreline. And I hear waves breaking." I nudged her shoulder. "Sit up. Land!"

Mirra opened her eyes. Her skin was blotchy, hair tangled, dark eyes sunken.

"There could be houses, Mirra. Phones. Food! Water! Get up!" I scooped up a handful of seaweed. "Look!"

She only moaned.

I grabbed my water bottle. "Mirra! Take a drink. Don't spill it." When she didn't reach for it, I helped her sit up. I held it, pouring the last tablespoon of my water into her mouth. She swallowed and moaned. "Feeling better?" Still no reply. "We're almost to land. People. Someone to help us."

Mirra hadn't moved. Even though my throat was desert dry, I kept talking. "I wonder how far north we've drifted. I see grass and, farther out, dunes." The ocean was shallow and I could glimpse bottom. "A few minutes, and we can step out. I don't see any people or boats yet."

"L-land, Annie?"

"Yes." I had to concentrate to form words. "I might see seals. Yes! Over there." I pointed to my right. She didn't answer. I cupped my hands around my cracked lips. "Help! Is anyone there?" I scanned the land. "Please, anyone?"

I glanced anxiously at Mirra. "Hang on. Just another minute and we'll be on land." A black shape moved through the fog. Excitement surged through me. Was it an animal? A human? It stepped out of the fog. "Mirra, a horse. Horses mean people!"

"Come on," I continued. "Let's jump out. It's shallow enough." I threw one leg over the side and splashed out into the knee-high water. "Please, Mirra," I said, pulling the raft onto the beach. "Look. It's land."

Mirra lifted her head.

I stretched my arms. "Oh, this feels so good. Come on, lean on me."

I hadn't counted on not being able to walk, and I swayed so much it took a long time to half-carry, half-drag Mirra out of the raft and onto the beach. A pile of plastic bottles and tangled net gave me hope. Litter meant people. "Sit and rest."

I managed to walk back, open the cooler, and pull out the two empty water bottles and put them in the cookie tin. Maybe I'd find enough water to fill all three. When I tried to walk back to Mirra, my knees buckled.

Mirra too, had sunk back onto the sand. I crawled a short way, but too slow. I forced myself to stand again. There. I waited until I was steady. Then I stumbled over to Mirra. I set the tin on the ground and pulled her to her feet. Two steps and she dropped back down. I had to leave her.

I took off both our life jackets ... tossed them on the shore, then on second thought, grabbed one to put under Mirra's head. I felt her forehead. Burning hot. "I'm going for people and water." I showed Mirra the tin. "You stay here. I'll be back soon."

A groan escaped my lips as I limped off into the dunes toward the rising sun and the seals. Not much to see besides sand, shrubs, and patches of grass.

Dunes to my left and right. Not a drop of fresh water anywhere. The breeze picked up and the late morning sun bore through the fog. I froze in my tracks. Mirra was out in the direct sun. Should I try to find her some shade? No, I'd hurry, find water, and get back to her.

One foot in front of the other, I told myself, my head throbbing. I swatted at the flies buzzing around my face and stumbled. I lay on the sand. The softness made me think of my bed at home and I just wanted to sleep. Sleep ... sleep ...

I jerked awake. Was that crying! Was I hearing Joey? My mind flashed to Mom's funeral when he'd cried so loudly my aunt had to take him away. But no. Fully awake now, I remembered. The cries were coming from gulls. Mirra! I'd left her.

Still early morning ... must have blacked out ... hurry ... have to get help ...

I staggered to my feet.

The horse, maybe the same one I'd seen from the raft, stood nearby. I stumbled toward it. A stallion. Mostly black but it had splashes of silver that made it seem almost magical. I had the feeling he was old. Old and wise. On his forehead was a white marking, shaped like a half moon. He seemed to be urging me to keep going.

"Do you know where fresh water is?" He walked down what appeared to be a path. I followed, stepping faster.

Grass rustled. I jerked my head toward the sound. "Help!" I called. "Is anyone there?" Silence. I trudged on.

The gnats followed me and I batted at them weakly. My guts twisted. Oh, yuck. I hurried for the bushes. I picked a few soft shrub leaves, and squatted, knees shaking. I grimaced as the gnats attacked. I ended up not being able to go and wished I hadn't wasted the energy.

Wearily, I shooed away the bugs, retrieved the tin, and returned to the horse. He plodded farther in and I followed. I told myself to remember landmarks so I could find my way back to Mirra. Mirra, I remembered. I'd left her out in the burning sun.

A fringe of tall grass hid my view of the seals, but I sometimes heard their barks. How many more steps could I take? I'd count them to keep myself going. I would only make myself walk 100 steps. No more.

The horse and I kept plodding through sand flats. At step ninety-two, I followed him past white and blue flowers. Past a mare and foal. To greener plants. And just ahead—cattails. And a pond!

"Ha-hahhhh!" I called, running. Water! "Thank you," I whispered to the horse as I cupped a handful and brought it close to my lips. I was about to suck up a mouthful, then stopped. What was floating in here? Horse prints surrounded the pond. Had they been stepping into the water? Could it have horse poop in it? I didn't care. I couldn't wait any longer.

I brought my dripping hand closer to my lips. *Never drink water from a stagnant pond. Boil it first.* Dad's words spoken on one of our camping trips were so real I mumbled, "O-kay." I couldn't drink, but I could bathe. I shed my shirt and borrowed pants and waded in, rubbing the water on my salt-crusted face and arms. I knew I had to get back to Mirra, but I couldn't help enjoying the cool water for a moment.

After I dressed, I searched for the horse. Gone. I scrubbed the tin with sand, rinsed it twice, then filled it and the empty water bottles with pond water.

Hiking back to Mirra, I scanned the distant dunes and valleys. "Help!" I hollered, my voice cracking. "Is anyone here? Please help us!"

A seal sunning itself on the beach raised its head to study me. Small birds sang. Could I find a rock and kill birds, pluck and roast them? I stumbled on.

When I returned to the raft, Mirra lay motionless. How many hours had she cooked in the sun? I sank alongside her. "Open your eyes, Mirra. Wake up. I found water. We have to make a fire. Boil it first." I held Mirra's head up, and she mumbled something. When I stopped holding her head, it fell back down.

Hurry, hurry, I chanted as I collected dry driftwood and a piece of dead shrub to help start the fire. I dug a hole in the sand and dragged the cooler close to it. Thankfully, we had matches. Pretty soon, I had a flame. I kept feeding the fire, but as I turned away, a blast of wind sent a heavy spray of sand toward the flame. For a moment, I thought it might still burn, but it flickered once, and went out. I forced myself to strike another match and start again. *You're almost there.*

I blocked the wind with the cooler and my body this time. The flame grew. Quickly, I set the tin with the pond water on top of the building flames.

I looked around at our makeshift camp, lit up by the orange light. Sand rippled across my feet, almost as if the land was breathing, as if it was alive.

CHAPTER EIGHT
THE LAND SPEAKS

R emembering how good it felt to bathe, I dribbled some precious water on Mirra's face. She murmured and raised her head. "I'll look around while the water boils," I told her, glancing at the tin setting on the burning sticks. "Make sure the fire keeps going, okay?"

"If ... goes out?"

"Add these bits of bark and driftwood."

"After it boils, drink?" Mirra's huge brown eyes moistened.

I nodded. Mirra closed her eyes. I forced myself to stand. Trying to find the strength I needed, I stared down at Mirra. She and I had met on the first day of second grade. That night, I'd told Mom I'd met a girl with pretty brown eyes and I wanted her to be my best friend. Mirra and I *had* been best friends.

For Mirra's ninth birthday, her mom, a dancer turned aerobic instructor, took both of us to the aquarium. I decided I wanted to train dolphins or be the diver who got to feed the sea turtles. I'd read a ton of books about marine biologists and marine life. Now, as I checked the horizon for boats, and looked up and down the beach seeing nothing but grass and sand, I wished I'd have spent more time reading sur-

vival books and paying attention during Beetle-
eater's shows.

Beyond tired, I jerkily set off toward high dunes
in the west. A band of horses trotted off to my left.
Not a fence in sight. This place reminded me of Isle
Royale. Was it an island?

I felt dizzy and beyond thirsty. I had to stop a minute and close my eyes. When I opened them, the
black and silver horse stood on top of a dune. He
seemed to be watching me. Had he seen people be-

fore? How had he come to this place? I thought of one of my favorite books, *Misty of Chincoteague*. In it, people herded horses from the island through the water to the mainland, where people bid on any they wanted to adopt. We couldn't be anywhere near Virginia, but wherever we were, this horse was definitely running free.

As I watched the horse, a sense of my mom's presence surrounded me. I shook my head, trying to clear it, but the feeling stayed. Could Mom have been reincarnated? Mom could be here, showing herself through this strong horse, this stallion, giving me strength to go on.

His forehead's crescent shaped blaze reminded me of the moon I'd seen last night from the sea. Sea Stallion, I silently named him. Thank you for helping me.

Suddenly, he galloped off, scaring a flock of birds with red beaks.

Terns, I realized. They landed in a green patch. Eggs? A hundred or so steps to find out.

Tee-aar! the birds sang. Nests! Several of them. Female terns watched me as I approached. I stepped toward the nearest nest. The female took flight. Three eggs! Smaller than chicken eggs, I'd grabbed all three when *Thwack!* The tern's beak nailed my scalp.

"Owww!" I yelled, scooting away. I set the eggs down to touch my head. I looked up and saw the bird circling above my head.

I hadn't come this far to let a measly bird scare me off. I shed my mom's fleece jacket, spread it out, and set the eggs safely on top. I took a few deep breaths and ran toward another nest. I grabbed two eggs and was running for the jacket-basket when the tern struck. "Ow!"

I rubbed my scalp, but I needed to keep going. Two more eggs without a strike, then three eggs costing me a bloodied scalp. By the time I'd cleaned out five nests, my scalp was wet and sticky.

I held the jacket-basket closed and hurried back to Mirra.

"Food!" I shouted. But Mirra didn't answer. "Eggs, Mirra." I ran to her and knelt at her side. "Sit up. And the water's boiling. We can drink. Open your eyes!"

When she didn't, I dropped to my knees. *Please still be alive. Don't die and leave me here all alone.*

She opened her eyes a slit.

"Mirra! I'm... I'm getting you a cup of water." I dashed to the cooler and found the stack of green plastic cups. Using the tail of my shirt for a hot pad, I picked up the tin and quickly filled a cup with boiling water. After pouring it back and forth into another cup, the water cooled down. "Sit up, Mirra." I used the voice that got Joey to take his medicine.

Mirra slowly obeyed. Dried blood crusted her lips. I steadied the cup. "It's cool enough," I promised, bringing it to her lips. Very carefully, I poured a small amount of water into Mirra's mouth.

Mirra sputtered and coughed. "M-more," she said. "I want more."

"Just half a cup for now. It's better to go slow so it stays down."

Mirra held the cup like it was crystal and drank. She passed the cup to me. "Your turn."

I refilled it. The warm water soothed my throat, and I kept it in my mouth a moment before swallowing. *Thank you, island horse.* As I looked at it, I felt Mom's presence again.

I started a second cup cooling, added more driftwood to the fire, then carefully set the eggs in the steamy water. I hoped the eggs were fresh. If we cracked them open to find half-formed chicks, I'd lose it.

"Where'd you find water?" Mirra asked.

"By a pond close to that patch of tall grass. We can wash in it too. Won't that feel good?"

"People?" Mirra swiveled her head. "Houses?"

"No, I haven't seen anybody yet. There are horses, though. Maybe there's a stable nearby." But I was doubting it. No homes or barns around and shoreline in every direction. The moist air too, made me strongly suspect we'd landed on an island.

Guessing the eggs were cooked enough, I used the green cup to scoop them out of the water. While they cooled on Mirra's jacket, I poured the clean water into the stackable cups. Finally, I emptied the pond water from the water bottles into the tin to start a new batch boiling.

And now, to eat! "Mmmm," I groaned, "these smell wonderful."

"Not hungry."

My head whipped around to stare at her. "No, you have to be hungry. You're just so sick you don't know it. You said you'd been dieting before this. That probably makes you especially weak. Eat a little, and I'm sure you'll feel better."

Not able to wait any longer, I burned my fingers peeling the shell of one. With my back to Mirra, I split it in half and peeked at what was inside. No half-cooked chick, thank goodness. I held out a piece for Mirra. Her hand flopped, though. Afraid she'd drop the precious egg in the sand, I said, "Open your mouth."

She did. The smell of the cooked eggs made my stomach growl. Taking my bite, I let the moist egg white and the soft yolk rest in my mouth. So good. I finished my egg and quickly peeled two more. Mirra could hold them herself. I nearly ate the next egg in one bite.

"Annie?" Mirra's voice was barely a whisper.

"Uh-huh."

"I'm sorry."

I held my breath.

When I didn't answer, she said, "For how I treated you. Freezing you out."

You not only froze me out, I wanted to say, *you cast me away. Like garbage in the ocean.*

"Annie?"

"I was in a bathroom stall the night of the first basketball game." I wiped my eyes. "I heard you tell Brittany about the bodysuit."

Mirra sat up straighter. "You were there?"

I nodded. Keep breathing and I'll get through this.

"Oh, no."

Is that all she could say? My adrenaline spiked, and I felt sick to my stomach. "You told her I needed to get a clerk to cut me out of the bodysuit and then you two laughed."

Mirra moaned. "It was stupid and mean, and I don't blame you for being mad. But you hurt me too." She kept looking at me. "There was your snort at my dragon comment. 'Oh, Mirra,' you laughed, and shot back something about my being such a little kid. And when I tried to talk to you about my plans after high school, you said something about my wanting to be only a hairdresser. Just because hairdressers don't go to college for four years doesn't mean they're stupid."

I shifted uneasily. I probably had said those things.

"And one more thing," Mirra said. "Kids get the idea you think you're better than them, and they don't like it. You'd have more friends if you didn't come across like a know-it-all."

We stared at each other for a long time. Mirra was the first to break the silence. "Whew! I feel better." Mirra smiled. "I needed to get that out. You too?"

I stood up, my stomach roiling. Seconds later, I hurried to the bushes, bent over, and vomited.

"Annie!" Mirra hurried toward me. "Are you okay?"

I wiped my mouth with the back of my hand. "Either the eggs are bad or I ate that last one too soon after drinking water." I straightened. Such a waste.

"You should try to eat that last egg," Mirra said. "You need something in your stomach."

I nodded to her. I slowly peeled the final egg. "I'm sorry," I said, meeting her gaze. "I can see where that hurt. I'm glad we got all this out." I took small bites of the egg. This time it stayed down.

Finally, I leaned my back against a small log near the campfire.

Darkness fell. Mirra could barely help me spread our jackets on the sand near the fire. What if she didn't survive the—? No! I wouldn't even think it.

Remember to get up, check on her, and add fuel, I told myself. I stretched out on the sand and gave in to exhaustion.

I woke up twice, listened to make sure Mirra was breathing, and added more wood to the fire. When squawking gulls announced it was morning, I muttered, "Could it only be day five?"

I sat up and watched the sunrise. The summer before third grade, my family rented a cabin near Bar Harbor. I'd invited Mirra. We'd gotten up at 4:00 a.m. so Dad could drive us to the top of Cadillac Mountain, where we'd be the first people in the continental United States to see the sunrise. I wished I could hold that special early morning in my mind, drawing strength from it, but when I stood up, feeling sore and achy, the memory vanished.

The gulls called again. Ever since I was a little kid, I'd fed the neighborhood gulls bread and other goodies. I wished that, by simply picturing the beach by my house, I could transport myself there.

But hearing an unfamiliar sound, rustling, made me whip my head around. People? My heart thumped madly as I scanned the area. Wild dogs? Coyotes? I searched for a stick to use for a weapon. Not finding any, I felt in my pocket for the knife.

Wrrrr! Small birds flitted from a patch of bushes.

I let out my breath and kept pretending I was home. I pictured the sparrow nest I'd found under our grill. Our grill. Chicken, steak, and burgers. Salad bowl loaded with tomatoes, carrots, and crunchy cucumbers. Gingerbread for dessert.

Mirra jerked to her feet with a shriek. "Something crawled across my face!"

A ghost crab half the size of my palm scurried toward its hole, its stalked eyes rotating to keep track of us.

"Yuck!" Mirra rubbed at her face. "I *hate* crabs. They're so... so crabby!"

Before I could stop myself, I giggled. The giggle turned into a laugh, sounding almost hysterical.

"You okay?" Mirra asked.

Wiping my eyes, I nodded. I scanned the shoreline near our raft and the horizon. Nothing. My stomach demanding food, I had a sudden thought. "Help me catch some crabs." I pointed to the twenty or so holes around us. "We'll have them for breakfast."

I expected Mirra's usual *Eww*, but when she didn't whine, I realized just how hungry she was. *Keep going*, I commanded myself. I added more wood to the fire and set the tin on top. "We need more water too," I said.

Mirra started following me, holding up her mom's jeans. "Hang on. I want to change."

After, we walked east toward the seals along the high-water mark. "There's one." I chased the yellowish-white crab, but it scooted into its hole before I could catch it.

Steven and I used to hunt ghost crabs by moonlight. One night, we caught a dozen or so. He leaped for them, once ending up with a face full of sand.

Minutes passed before we saw another one. The crab's hole was only one step from my right foot. It scurried, but I was faster. My hand shot out and closed on its body. It tried pinching me, but I didn't drop it.

"Bring the pot," I called, realizing I should have brought a container. Once at camp, I threw the scrapping crab in the tin of near-boiling water and then grabbed all four cups for containers. Mirra tried to catch one, but she was too slow. Seeing her feeble attempt made me try even harder. By the time I had eight crabs cooked, Mirra had slumped down in the sand again. I held a crab up to my mouth and blew to cool it off. I also caught a whiff. Could we eat these smelly things?

"Crab in restaurants is expensive," I said, holding it out to Mirra.

She sat up and took it.

"We can pretend we're off on a double date," I said, hoping to perk her up. I took a crab, blew on it, then broke off a leg.

As I looked for meat to suck out, Mirra said, "Okay. Who are you with?"

I breathed through my mouth so I didn't have to smell the crab and sucked at the opening in the leg. I found a raisin-sized bite. "I'm with Nick," I finally said.

Mirra picked out some crab meat. "Nick's on the track team, right?"

"Uh-huh."

"Ever go out with him?"

When I was sure I could answer without my voice breaking, I said, "No. He told me his brother was picking up some kids to go to the Valentine dance, but I told him I couldn't go."

Mirra nodded and gazed off.

I reached in my pocket and pulled out the glittery hair clip. Amazing that I still had it. I swept up my hair and pinned it in place. Just for a moment, I wanted life to revolve around parties and boys.

"Ha!" Mirra exclaimed. "You stabbed a shark with a knife, but you're afraid to go out with a boy?"

I shrugged my shoulders. "That stuff doesn't come easy for me."

"If we ever get off this island, you should practice. Make small talk with strangers. Eventually try it out on boys."

I nodded.

"Okay," Mirra said, "I'm with Ryan and you're with Nick. We're wearing shimmery dresses and the guys are in tuxes. The outside trees are decorated in white lights, and it's snowing. Can you see it?"

"I see it." I'm in an emerald dress and my hair clip glitters in the lights. "It sounds beautiful." I sigh. "Then what?"

"Nick pulls your chair out for you. Ryan hands me a pink rose. We sit at a table lit by a chandelier and sip water from a crystal glass."

"The waiter sets down a fancy plate full of delicious looking crabs," I add. "Mmm, they smell so good."

Mirra and I both took a crab. We twisted off a leg and brought the food toward our mouths.

CHAPTER NINE
DISCOVERIES

I swallowed the crab meat. The image of me in the emerald dress at a fancy restaurant faded fast, and I nearly gagged on the smelly, rubbery meat. Still, I knew I had to eat so I finished my share.

"I'm still hungry," Mirra said.

"Me too." I gathered up all the crab parts that weren't edible and tossed them toward the terns' nests. I caught a whiff of my smelly hands and longed for soap. I pictured our bathroom with its big fat bar of soap.

Were Dad and the boys searching anywhere near here? Was the Coast Guard still looking for us? The wind gusted, and I zipped up Mom's fleece. I found a few stray horse hairs from when she'd worn it while helping at Grandma and Grandpa's horse farm. I was about to pick them off when I thought of how Sea Stallion had led me to water. I let the hairs stay.

"Let's see what else we can find to eat," I said. "We have to get to know this place and figure out a way to signal for help." I guessed it would take most of a day to walk the whole length of the island, so we'd have to check it out in sections.

"Do you think a boat will come for us today?" Mirra wiped her hands on her jeans.

"Maybe. We need to be ready, keep the fire going, and start another one. It'd be good to have a bunch of signal fires ready."

"Can we make one of the new fires in a place without crabs and sleep there tonight?"

"We can try," I said. Mirra must have wanted it badly, because she didn't complain about the walk. When we found a spot without any signs of crabs, we dug a second fire pit, gathered driftwood and tinder, carried the burning stick over to start it, then dragged the cooler. Trying to help our moods, I said, "We can call this camp No Crabs Allowed."

Mirra smiled.

"Do you have enough energy to explore with me? Maybe we'll find signs of people."

Mirra shrugged. "I'll try."

Mirra and I headed east. "We need Nick here," Mirra said. "He's a long-distance runner, right?"

"Uh-huh, he could cover this island in a few minutes." I shaded my eyes, trying to get my bearings.

"These dunes are something else," Mirra said. "Wouldn't Steven or Ryan have fun ripping around here in a dune buggy?"

I nodded. Only a few bushes, one tree, and no rocks to get in their way. I groaned. What I'd give to hear a dune buggy right now.

"Look at all this junk!" Mirra pointed to scattered bottles, pieces of nets, chunks of metal, ropes, poles and pieces of canvas. "Do you think this means people live here?" She picked up a plastic bottle.

I hated to dash Mirra's hopes, but I had to be honest. "It looks washed in to me."

"Maybe we aren't far from the mainland." She bit her lip.

I had no idea how far we'd drifted or where we were. "In case we don't find people right away, we should work on a shelter. That canvas might work." I pointed.

"I hope we don't have to spend another night out here." Mirra's voice cracked.

"Can you make it up this dune so we can look around?" When Mirra groaned, I added, "With luck we'll see a house and be back home by suppertime."

Either the word *house* or *suppertime* made Mirra pick up the pace. The sand was soft. For every step up, we slid halfway back down, but eventually we were high enough to stop and take a look around. I drew in a deep breath, held it, and shaded my eyes with my hand.

North, south, east, and west. Dunes, some tall grasses, a few shrubs, but no houses. Endless ocean rolling in, slapping the shore with waves. Gulls swooped all around us, their cries sounding like taunting laughter. Home for supper. Right.

"It *is* an island," Mirra said, her voice choked with disappointment. "Nothing but an island."

I swallowed a sob. "Come on." I forced myself to be positive. "Let's make a map, plot out where we

landed, and plan where we should set up signal fires."
I smoothed the sand and then, using my finger, drew
the island. "This place is shaped like a banana with
its ends sticking up."

"Or a boat, a lifeboat."

"Yeah, okay. We landed in the middle toward the
bottom of the boat, the south." I made an X.

Mirra pointed to the left. "The tern nests and the
high dune are to the west."

"The east is greener with the valley and pond." I
pointed.

Mirra nodded.

"If a boat comes, we want them to see our smoke,
so we should set up three or four signal fires at
different places."

Mirra stood holding her stomach. "Can't we try to
find some food first?"

"Yeah, okay." We'd been walking and searching
for several minutes when a rustling sound in the tall
grasses made me freeze. The wind, for once, wasn't
blowing. Was an animal moving and making that
sound? Would it be an animal we could catch, cook,
and eat?

I was still thinking about the sound when I
nearly stepped on a little red strawberry. "Mirra,
look!" I dropped down to the sand and popped one of
the tiny berries into my mouth. "Mmmm. Good."

We picked and ate all we could find. Not hearing any more unusual noises, I let myself relax. "Let's keep looking."

When I spotted plants with little green pods, I shrieked, "Over here. I think these are wild peas."

"Peas grow wild?"

"I think so." I split open the pod, smelled the small pea, and placed it on my tongue. "Mmm, it's good." I ate the whole thing, pod and all.

Mirra picked one. She nibbled on a pea, then ate the whole thing too.

Once we'd eaten all we could find, I remembered the fire. Shedding my fleece, I said, "Help me find some dry wood."

I filled the jacket with driftwood and Mirra carried a few pieces too. Our first fire by the raft was out, and the fire at "No Crabs Allowed" camp was nearly out. I quickly added a few smaller pieces of driftwood to it.

"Someone just has to come for us today," Mirra said, looking out at the water.

"If we stay busy, the time will go by faster. Let's stack bark and driftwood by both fires, so if we see a helicopter or boat we can signal it. If you get the small stuff, I'll get driftwood."

"Can you do both?" Mirra looked toward the pond. "I want to go wash off in the pond like you did."

"I only dunked myself." I stopped myself from adding, *It wasn't as if I soaked in a bubble bath.*

A mouse skittered across the sand and ran toward the bushes. My mind flashed back to another mouse ... and three babies ... just a month ago. Dad had discovered them in the corner near our garage. "Look at this," he'd called to me. The mother had chewed through a thick rag and itchy insulation to make a comfy nest. All that effort to take care of the little ones.

I glanced at Mirra's tiny, slumped shoulders and sunken eyes. "Go ahead," I said. "Bring back some water, though, okay?"

My whole body ached, but I forced myself to break up the wood, then go off searching for more.

I found some large driftwood pieces that looked like they might have been part of a dock and a bunch of smaller scraps. My first pile of firewood was nearly the size of a muskrat lodge by the time Mirra returned, her hair dripping.

She handed me the tin of water. "I shouldn't have left the cover behind. Half of the water sloshed out."

Exactly. I clenched my jaw. Deep breath. "Well, one signal fire's set to go." My stomach rumbled. "I've been thinking. Maybe we could rig up a fishing pole or look for oysters. Oysters seem easier. They need to attach to something, though, like a log. Have you seen any logs in the water?"

"No." Mirra sank onto the sand.

Was she truly exhausted and sick, or was she happy to let me do all the work? I silently counted to ten. "I know you're tired, but you have to help. The day's half gone."

"I'm afraid to look for oysters. The water might get too deep. Remember, I can't swim."

Deep breaths. Again. "Okay. How about if you gather more wood and keep an eye on the fire."

She mumbled something in a tone that made me mad, but then I reminded myself of how weak she was and how she'd nearly died. "Or if you'd rather get tern eggs, that'd be a big help. Just watch out because they'll dive-bomb you."

I'd barely left Mirra when a flash of movement in the dunes made me turn to look. Sea Stallion, patches of his silvery coat flashing in the morning sun, stopped to look at me. If only I could talk to him, ask him questions. *How did you end up here? Do people come and check on you?* Another horse snorted in the distance, and Sea Stallion trotted off in that direction.

I scanned the ocean, staring longest toward the west, toward home. If I was back in Friendly, I might be thinking about something fun, like making a YouTube video. I could do one on how to gather and prepare oysters. I'd get the boys and Ryan to recreate the time we'd peeled a bunch of oysters off the support legs of a pier, washed and shucked them, and then deep-fried them. I'd include Ryan dipping his oyster into his mom's special sauce. Ryan ... He didn't know it, but he was the reason I was stuck here.

I had to stay focused on finding food. Oysters on my mind, I walked along the shore. There! A submerged log. And what was that? A group of seals lazing nearby. I took off my shoes, socks, and jeans before stepping into the water. Seals wouldn't be so relaxed if sharks were in the area. Still, I knew, sharks could move fast. I looked around for any telltale fins as I waded farther out.

The strong surf meant I had to use my arms for balance. The waves splashed my face but I reached the log. I felt around and, after a few minutes, I had my first oyster. Then a second. Then a third! I headed back to shore.

Mirra was on her way back too, and she was carrying her jacket like it held eggs. Once by the fire, she set it down carefully and took off her cap. "Talk about vicious!" she exclaimed. She touched her scalp gently and laughed. "Next time we ought to wear the tin on our heads."

I pictured Mirra with a cookie tin on her head and silently laughed, but it wasn't a bad idea. "How many did you get?"

"Seven."

Not too bad.

Mirra set the eggs in the boiling water, and I placed the oysters around the fire. "Any sign of people?" I asked.

Mirra shook her head. "Just a bunch of seals."

"I saw seals too." Would we be able to hunt one or butcher it with only our small knife? I hoped we wouldn't be here long enough to have to find out. My mouth watered. "Have you ever eaten oysters raw?"

"No," Mirra answered. "But my dad ordered them once when we were out."

It was easy to picture Mirra and her parents in a fancy restaurant with crystal chandeliers, but as soon as I looked at Mirra's red, blistered and peeling face, the image faded.

My guts twisted, letting me know it was time to try going to the bathroom again. I handed Mirra the knife. "The oysters might pop open once they're steamed, but here's the knife in case you need it. I'll be right back; I have to go to the bathroom."

I returned to find Mirra bent over the knife. "I broke the blade," she said.

"You didn't!" Heat rose to my face. I couldn't look at her. An inch of the blade tip was broken off. It was barely still usable.

I knew I was going too far, but I couldn't stop myself. I spun around to face her. "This is our only knife. We can't get another one!"

Mirra covered her ears. "Don't screech like that! You sound like the gulls." She uncovered her ears and barked back at me. "You aren't perfect, you know.

You dropped my phone. You let it get swept out to the sea, and no one knows where we are."

"A wave washed your phone away," I shouted. "It wasn't my fault." I stomped off.

Minutes passed, then rustling in the grass made me wonder if Mirra was following me. No, I could see her off in the distance. Whatever was moving in the grass, it sounded big. Sea Stallion? No, I'd be able to see him. I crept closer to the rustling. If it was a small animal, like a rabbit, could we set a snare and catch it?

A ribbon of green rippled along the ground, but it dipped into a valley so I couldn't see it clearly. Next time I'd have to be faster.

I did find a great pile of dry wood and, willing to return to *Just-a-Knife Mirra*, I grabbed an armful. I set it down near the fire.

The oysters had steamed open, and I pulled them out of the fire. I slid Mirra's portion toward where she sat on the log. I couldn't bring myself to hand them to her. I popped one open and inspected it. The grayish meat had a gristly looking part and folds at one end. It didn't look appetizing, but it was food. I opened my mouth as wide as I could without causing my cracked lips to bleed. "Mmm," I said, my mood brightening. "Not bad."

"Tastes like saltwater," Mirra said, but she popped open a second one.

We finished the oysters, then shared the boiled eggs and the water. I was no longer angry, but I was still hungry. I stared out at the ocean. At home, I had loved watching the rolling surf and the changing colors of water and sky. Now the ocean scene looked only endless.

Mirra turned to me. "Annie?" Her voice was so soft I had to lean forward to hear. "Have you ever been ... hungry like this before?"

"No." My voice trembled.

"I haven't either." Mirra turned to face me head on. "Tell me the truth. Do you think we're going to be rescued?"

Answering No might make her realize she had to help me with food, fire, and shelter, but I couldn't crush her hopes. "I think it's a good sign that horses live on this island. And one of them, Sea Stallion I call him, seems friendly." I didn't tell her how he'd led me to water, and I was too embarrassed to say how I was drawn to him because he made me think of Mom.

Mirra looked in their direction. "I haven't paid much attention to the horses. But maybe somebody comes to check on them." She rubbed her sunburned nose.

I knew from the tightness and pain that my fairer skin must look even worse than hers. I grabbed the tin and its cover. "We need to keep thinking survival; starting with getting more water." I walked toward the pond and Mirra followed. While we refilled our bottles and the tin, two black ducks flushed from cattails. At nearly the same time, hooves thundered toward us. I held my breath.

A muddy yellow horse led a band of mares and foals past us to a grassy area. "Sea Stallion isn't in this group," I said. "I wonder if he has his own band."

"He's the friendly one, the one you saw yesterday," Mirra recalled, more to herself than to me. "Yesterday's a blur." Her eyes had dark circles underneath. She was watching the muddy, muscular stallion circle five mares and two foals. "They're a weird color, aren't they?"

"Uh-huh, and kind of small."

The horses continued to clip grass, chew it slowly, and watch us.

"Remember that time in fourth grade when you brought me to your grandparents' ranch?" Mirra asked.

I nodded, remembering the two of us grooming Tex and Sarge. Mirra had been too scared to try riding. I thought about Grandma and Grandpa. They were probably with Dad, helping the family get through this.

I inched closer to the horses. If they didn't shy away, that could mean they were used to people. When I was near enough to see the yellow stallion's scars, his ears flickered. He arched his neck and tail and shook his golden mane. *Phruuuu!* He stomped his foot, blew air loudly through his nostrils again, and squealed a warning.

"Watch out!" Mirra cried.

But the stallion shook his mane and turned away. I *won't charge you now*, his body language said, *but I'm going to keep my eye on you.* He trotted off and his band followed.

"Muscle Boy's not very friendly," Mirra said, bringing me back to the present.

"No, he reminds me of Sophia Putman."

"Who?"

"This snotty girl who joined the youth group a few months ago. She and her friends think they're so cool with their cute clothes and jazzy—" I stopped, feeling my face turn red. I slyly glanced at Mirra, but she was still watching the horses. Did she have a clue how I saw her and Brittany? Did she care?

"Let's climb that dune." I pointed to a group of dunes on the eastern end. "And scope things out again. We might have missed something last time."

"Please," Mirra said, following me, "let there be people with food, water, and phones."

We picked the route with the firmest sand and reached the top. I still couldn't find a single sign of human life.

I guessed the island was twenty miles long and only a mile or so wide.

"There's the pond where we bathed," Mirra said, pointing, "but past our camp there's another one. It's more like a lake."

"You're right. Maybe it's cleaner. Want to walk that far and check it out?"

"We can try."

On the way, we found another strawberry patch and ate every red berry. We were north of our camp near shore when we passed what could be clam flats. "The tide's going out. After we check out the lake, we can come back here and see if we can get some clams."

"Let's hurry. I really need some food."

We reached the top of another dune. The lake shimmered below. It looked less weedy than the pond, and would probably be cleaner for drinking and bathing. Tall grasses and bushes surrounded it. Something large moved through. I tried to make it out. A fox or coyote? I hoped it wasn't a wolf. When we reached the lake, I looked for tracks. When I found them, I sucked in a sharp breath. Not an animal. These were *human* footprints!

CHAPTER TEN
SCAVENGERS

I stood frozen, staring at the footprint. I searched the landscape. Was there someone watching us right now?

"What is it?" Mirra asked.

"Someone else is here. Someone who's not wearing shoes and has man-sized feet." I glanced at the tallest vegetation. "I've seen the grass rippling when there hasn't been any wind." An icy chill snaked down my spine. "I think someone's hiding from us."

Mirra pivoted. "Why would they hide?"

"I ... I don't know. It could be an escaped convict or a drug runner. Maybe we don't," I swallowed hard, "want to find him."

"Calm down," Mirra said. "It could also be someone who could help us, someone with a phone."

"But if it's someone like that, why hasn't he already helped?" My voice rose in panic. "He has to know we're here."

We followed the prints for several minutes until they stopped at the hard-packed sand. We looked in all directions. Mirra looked dazed. "I feel dizzy."

"We need to eat. Let's head to the clam flats." I took her arm. "We should also start carrying the knife and something like a rock."

Mirra nodded.

With every step, I was on high alert for any sound or movement. Was he watching us? "The watcher," I whispered. Was he hiding behind that clump of bushes? In the tall grass near the north shore?

We didn't find even one rock, but Mirra found a knife-like stick, which she put in her pocket.

At the clam flats, I said, "Look for clams shooting out water and making spout marks."

"Spout marks?"

"Uh huh. They're the size of a nickel. Or sometimes you can see the clams' little streams of water."

After a few minutes of searching, Mirra clapped like a little kid. "Here's one shooting out water! And there's another one."

"Good job!" I dropped to my knees and frantically dug with my hands. Sand packed under my nails, but I kept digging. "Be quick, or they get away."

Mirra watched.

"Got it!" I clutched the clam, feeling my eyes well up with happy tears. Food. Wonderful food.

Mirra pitched in and together we dug up sixteen clams. She grimaced at her dirty nails with their chipped black polish. "We should carry the oyster shells and use them for mini shovels."

I blinked in surprise. "That's a good idea."

As we crossed the dunes to return to our camp, I kept thinking about the footprints. Someone was probably watching us. My breathing became quick gasps as I looked all around. There! Behind that bush! Was that a person crouching? I patted my pocket and felt the broken knife. Holding it by my side, I crept up to the tall grasses, but didn't see anything unusual.

As the clams baked in the flames, I kept alert, whipping around at the slightest noise. But when no one appeared, I finally pocketed the knife.

Mirra poured cups of hot water from the tin. "Remember how we put on that play for our parents and pretended to be sophisticated, rich ladies? We poured tea afterward." Mirra's grin was infectious. "Shall we dine on clams this noon, my dear Miss Bardo?"

"Ah, yes." I waved in what I hoped was a dainty, ladylike gesture.

"Such a dilemma." Mirra tilted her chin up. "On the half-shell or steamed in champagne?"

"I ... I'm not sure."

"I'm thinking champagne," Mirra announced, flicking her hair out of her eyes. "I shall carry my Gucci handbag and wear the sapphires. I do hope our private jet is available." She curtsied.

I attempted to curtsy too, but my legs got tangled. An unfamiliar sound sprang from me. A full out laugh.

When gulls shrieked at something in the tall grass, though, I furtively watched. Who was out there?

Mirra handed me a plate of steamed clams. It was tricky using the broken blade to open the first one, but I eventually managed and handed Mirra the knife.

As I chewed on the flavorless, rubbery pieces, I thought of other times Mirra and I had put on plays. Mirra's mom had a storage box filled with wigs, dress-up clothes, and props. Back then, I hadn't stressed about my looks or the fact that I wasn't as tiny as Mirra. I'd put on a short curly wig or a fake rhinestone tiara and think I was beautiful. Mom recorded one of our shows. Two years ago, we'd grabbed chips and sodas and watched it, laughing all the while.

I watched as Mirra tried to pry open her clam with the jagged blade. Mirra and I would never be friends like that again. As much as I wished we could return to that time, I had to be realistic. This was our new reality.

Sparrows flitted off as if spooked. I spun around and searched. The watcher?

"See anything?" Mirra asked.

"No." When I could breathe normally again, I answered, "Help me think this through. If that footprint means someone's here, where could he be hiding?"

"Almost anywhere," Mirra said, "but it'd be easiest to hide in Green Valley."

"Right. It has all those bushes." I thought a minute longer. "The watcher might try to grab our raft. We should bring it closer."

We headed to the middle of the south shore. The sunlight was fading, but we were close to where we'd left the raft. "I think it should be around here."

Mirra shrugged. "I was so sick when we landed, I don't remember where we were."

We kept searching. I was beyond hungry and tired and Mirra stumbled so often I worried she'd collapse. Finally, I recognized our first fire pit. I looked around. No raft in sight.

We kept looking. "Either the watcher took it," I said, "or the tide did."

"You didn't bring it up on shore far enough." Her tone cut like jagged glass.

"Ha, you're blaming me?" I was past the point of caring what came out of my mouth. "I was busy taking care of you, you st—" I clamped my jaws shut.

"What?" she glared at me. "Stupid idiot?"

"You said it. Not me."

She stormed off.

Be that way! I'd had enough. Mirra could wander off alone. I was staying at camp.

As I added fuel to the fire, I imagined our raft bobbing in the endless ocean. With it gone, there was no escape. We could be stuck here together for the rest of our lives.

Chapter Eleven
Help!

A s darkness approached, the temperature plummeted. Mirra had left hours ago. My anger over her blaming me for the missing raft switched to worry. Could the watcher have grabbed her? I'd build up the fire and then search for her.

While I was gathering dry firewood, I saw her return to camp. I joined her, not saying a word, simply stacking the wood. She put the four terns' eggs she'd gotten into the tin of water. I'd need to get my own supper, maybe oysters.

I kept searching for strangers as I strode toward the oyster log, partially out of the water because of low tide. I found six oysters. I sat on the beach and ate them raw. The sunset put on an amazing show of oranges and reds, but I was too anxious to appreciate it. After chewing the last raw oyster, I wiped my smelly hands on my navy blue T-shirt. "Those clothes she wears," Brittany had said, that night in the bathroom.

Mirra had giggled, then she'd told about the bodysuit.

"Oh my God," Brittany had shrieked. "That is too funny!"

The memory should have seemed trivial. After all, back then I was fed, clean, had all the water I wanted, and I was safe. But it still hurt.

When I returned to camp, Mirra was sitting on a log. She glanced at me, and it could have been an opening, but I was still too mad to talk. I had taken off Mom's fleece, but now I put it back on. A wave of loneliness washed over me. Struggling not to cry, I glimpsed two horses near the beach, silhouetted in the moonlight. It was the palomino mare and her yearling. Mother and daughter. I wrapped my arms around myself.

As darkness surrounded me, I lay down. Day five, with its range of emotions, had been one of the longest I'd ever experienced.

I calculated the date as June 10th. Tomorrow would have been my parents' anniversary. My poor dad. Lost a wife and now a daughter.

I might have continued feeling sad and lonely, but a crab crawled on my arm. I was too slow to catch it for food. We wouldn't be able to call this "No Crabs Allowed Camp" anymore.

My skin itched from boils, mosquito bites, and whipping sand. Between that and the fear of creepy crabs, my anger at Mirra, and my worry about the watcher, I couldn't sleep. I heard Mirra rustling around a lot too. I vowed as soon as it got light, I'd figure out a shelter. Maybe I could solve one problem.

Cold wind gusts made me wrap my mom's fleece tighter around my body. I lay my cheek against its softness and pretended it was a hug, keeping me safe and warm. With that thought, I drifted off to sleep.

When I woke up, sand covered my face and body. The waves were crashing louder than I'd ever heard them and it was foggy, yet I somehow knew it was late morning, maybe almost noon. I couldn't believe I'd slept this long until I looked over at Mirra. Curled up in a ball, she still slept.

I heard a sound, like a man yelling, and I suddenly bolted up. That same sound, I now remembered, had woken me. The watcher?

"Mirra," I whispered, peering through the fog. "I hear something."

She didn't stir, and I had to talk louder over the sound of the waves. This time she sat up. I peered through the soupy mess.

I heard another sound. Was that a motor? A boat motor? What if rescuers had come? "BOAT! MIRRA! I hear a boat!"

"Me too. Hurry!" We ran toward the sound. A bright yellow dinghy. Maybe three people. Motoring away!

"Stop!" I screamed, but the surf drowned me out. Signal fire! "Keep calling!" I shouted to Mirra. "I'll build up the fire."

Mirra ran to shore, shouting. I sprinted to our fire and added driftwood. I couldn't see Mirra and her calls were faint over the sound of the motor. Would they hear her?

"Come on, fire!" I added small pieces of wood, then larger ones. "Come on!"

My uncle had a yellow dinghy. He and my dad and probably Mirra's dad would soon reach my uncle's red boat. Once onboard, they'd leave, either for home or to keep searching.

Hurry, fire! I added two more pieces of driftwood before running toward Mirra on shore. "They don't hear me!" she wailed.

I looked back. The fog sucked up the smoke and flames from our fire, but I could make out the outline of a big, red boat, the size and color of my uncle's. "Dad!" I shouted over the pounding waves and motor. "Dad!"

I peered through the fog. Were they lifting the dinghy and its motor on board? Would they circle around the island? I could start our other signal fires. They just had to see us!

"Keep calling. I'll start more fires." Even as I said it, I knew I'd be spending too much precious time running to each of the fires. Still, I had to try. At the second fire, I piled on tinder chanting, "Go, fire. Go!" I got a whisper of smoke before running to the third. I could no longer hear Mirra or see anything.

After I got the third fire going, I ran back to her. She was still calling, but now her voice was raspy.

"STOP!" I shouted. "STOP!"

The red boat seemed to be circling the island. The watcher! Would he try to signal it too? "Help add more wood to the fires," I called to Mirra. By the time we'd fed all three fires, long minutes had passed. The boat's motor revved up and Mirra and I stood in silence, watching it heading away ... away ... away.

Come back, I silently begged.

We stood a long time. Then Mirra held her stomach and doubled over as if in pain.

When the speck was no more, I sank onto my knees. I curled up into a ball like a scared little kid. We had missed our chance. Our one chance. We might not get another.

I tried to block out the pounding waves and protect myself from the whipping sand, but there was no stopping them. I hated the sounds of those waves constantly pounding in my ears, those waves that drowned out the sounds of our whimpers.

Hate filled my throat until it spilled out. I hated worrying about the watcher and whether the fire was still going. I hated salty spray coating my skin and clothes. I hated the fishy smell and the bites and sores and using leaves for toilet paper and always being hungry and thirsty and, I hated myself. If only I hadn't slept the morning away. If I'd stayed on watch, we'd be heading back home right now.

I looked at Mirra. She had collapsed near me. The cries erupting from her throat were more pitiful than any sound I'd ever heard. I couldn't comfort her, though. My own insides were too raw.

When I could finally speak, all I could say was, "I'm checking for prints."

I found three sets, two with tennis shoes, one with a boot heel. I curled up in the sand nearest the boot heel, knowing it was my dad's. I lay there a long time. Would he come again? Could I hope?

Hope, nothing but a four-letter word. Hope sets you up like a surfer's wave only to bang you against the rocks. It makes you believe things will get better, when they just get worse. *I am trying to do my best and you just keep pounding.*

My insides boiling with fury, I raised a fist and faced the waves. Well go ahead, I silently cried. I will not let you win. Not you or the fog or the wind or hunger or thirst.

I grabbed a handful of sand. I have news for you, waves. You thought I was tough before. You haven't seen anything yet. I stood up and whipped the sand at the ocean. I am done with sitting back and letting things happen to me. I will survive this. And Mirra will too. I'll make sure of it.

I joined Mirra on the sand near shore. She moaned. "Why didn't they stay longer?" Her voice sounded raw. "They knew it was foggy, that we couldn't see much."

I bit my lip. "They figured we weren't here and bad weather was coming." I nodded toward the rough ocean. "They knew they had to get out of here."

Mirra looked and then she covered her face with her hands. "I didn't sleep all night with the crabs and the cold so when I did fall asleep—"

"I know. Same with me." I shook my head. "Stupid." I saw Mirra tense and quickly added, "Stupid of us. We should have made sure one of us was alert."

Mirra's voiced cracked. "Do-do you think it was our parents?" Mirra choked.

"The dinghy was fluorescent yellow like the one my Uncle Jim has and ... I checked prints. A set of small and large tennis shoes, and prints like my ... like my dad's boots." I tried to swallow.

"Your uncle probably brought his big boat over and then stayed to watch Steven and Joey." Mirra seemed to withdraw like a hermit crab retracts to its shell. "Mom and Dad. Right here."

Had they gotten a map of the area and stayed at different ports? They might be planning to search a chunk of the coast. There wasn't any reason for them to come back a second time.

Long minutes passed. I managed one hopeful thought. "Maybe they'll find our drifting life raft, and they'll know to come back here. Mirra?" No answer. "We need to get a grip."

She groaned, "If they find our life raft, they'll think we drowned and stop searching."

I rubbed my forehead, feeling skin peel off.

Mirra stared out at the ocean. "Why is this happening to us? Why?"

I thought for a long time. "I don't know why bad things happen. They just do. We've survived six days. We can last another six."

Mirra and I struggled to stand. Together we stockpiled dry driftwood by the four signal fires so they'd be ready. Then we began work on a shelter. We found four poles in the debris pile, dragged them to camp, and using a chunk of driftwood, worked to pound them so they formed two upright Xs. As tired as I was, it felt good to build something.

I fit a fifth rail in the crook of the Xs and Mirra threw the canvas over the roof rail. Small, but it would help keep the crabs away and alert any rescuers that we were here.

"Annie," Mirra said, her forehead wrinkled. "The footprint person. Didn't he or she see the boat in time either? Otherwise, why didn't he call out?"

Something else I hadn't thought through. "I don't know, unless he doesn't want to be found, not by us or anyone else." The island breeze made the hairs on the back of my neck tingle. *Secrets*, the breeze seemed to whisper. *This island holds many secrets.*

CHAPTER TWELVE
STUPIDITY

Mirra and I sat down to share clams. Talking about missing our rescuers was too painful, so I shared a positive thought. "I've been thinking. The watcher could help us get rescued."

Mirra swallowed. "How's that?"

"We've only seen one set of footprints, so I'm betting he's here alone and since there isn't a boat, he might have made plans to have people pick him up. That'd be good news, unless," I hesitated, then figured it was better for Mirra to hear my fears, "unless the reason he hasn't shown himself is that he doesn't want us knowing what he's doing and he's planning on getting his partner to ... help get rid of us."

Mirra's eyes widened, and I wished I hadn't said anything.

"After we eat, let's look for more weapons. You know, rocks or poles we can sharpen. I'll try to find a sharp stick to carry like yours."

Mirra patted the pockets of her jeans. The tip of the stick stuck out. She wrapped her arms tighter around herself. She hated the fight scenes in movies and closed her eyes during any violent scenes.

After we set out, she said, "Maybe we'll find some more strawberries or peas. Hey, I forgot to tell you, I saw a sea turtle crawling up on shore yesterday."

"Really? Probably looking for a place to lay her eggs." I hated to think about killing it for turtle soup, but it was something to keep in mind. "If we find the eggs," I said, "we could cook a turtle omelet." It would probably taste like gamey Vaseline, but it would fill our bellies and be better than killing the turtle.

We found a sharp stick for me to carry, but didn't find any more strawberries or peas. Late in the day, I spied two long poles that had washed in. "Check these out. We can make our shelter bigger."

Back home, I studied our shelter. We stuck the poles in the sand raising the roof and making it roomier. At least one thing had gone right today.

Legs feeling heavy as posts, I did a final sunset search for a rescue boat. Walking in the twilight alone was so creepy, I quickly grabbed two extra poles, and hurried back. I refused to think about anything scary. Instead, I pictured how I would wittle the ends of these into spears so we'd have weapons if needed.

I set them near our tent, and then crawled inside along with Mirra. She was already asleep. Twenty-four hours ago, Mirra and I had fought. Our actions might have cost our lives, and I was determined to change. If we'd talked and worked together, we'd be home by now.

Without needing to worry about pesky crabs or the wind blowing sand, I should have gone right to sleep, but I kept imagining I heard shouts. *Annie! An-*

nie! Once I even left the tent and called out, waking Mirra. But no rescuers answered.

I woke up early. Day seven.

I'd held out talking about making a latrine, but since we might be here a while, Mirra and I made the clump of bushes north of camp our bathroom. I carried over an oyster shell so we'd be able to dig what my father called "cat holes." Next, I pocketed two more shells for digging clams, and we headed to the flats.

I'd thought about having us carry the extra poles for weapons, but I hadn't taken the time to sharpen the ends yet and we'd need our hands to carry back clams. My eyes kept shifting from watching for boats to watching for whoever had made the bare footprint. Once there, I said, "Let's set up another signal fire. It should be high enough that the tide won't wash it away."

By the time we'd gathered driftwood, the tide had gone out. When I spotted a clam shooting out a stream of water, I started digging. Mirra joined in. We each had a bunch of clams when a leaping shape offshore caught my eye. "Look!" A dolphin rose, arched its body, then dove back in. Seconds later, three more dolphins leaped. "They're playing."

We stood and watched the magical moment. "They sure are having fun," Mirra said a few minutes later. "Hey, we have so much food here, let's have a luau. Remember the one we had at the end of fifth grade?"

I nodded. "That cute guy, Ryder, cooked clams."

"Right. He wrapped them in seaweed and steamed them." Mirra scooped out another clam. "You want to do that?"

I grinned. "I know where there's plenty of seaweed."

While the clams roasted in seaweed, I tied a chunk of netting to the inside of our tent-shelter. We could keep a few pieces of firewood up there and always have dry wood.

We liked the clams' saltier flavor and decided we'd fix them this way again. Shortly after we'd finished eating, Mirra took off for the pond. Goldilocks, the palomino, and her yearling trotted past. Goldilocks saw me and stopped. I slowly approached. Goldilocks glanced at her colt, then at me. I got within an arm's length, stopped, and held out the grass. When Goldilocks didn't move, I blew gently in her face, *hello* in horse language.

I smiled when she blew back. "I'm glad to meet you too. And you," I said, turning to the little one. The yearling sniffed at me. I reached toward him.

He turned his neck toward his mother as if asking permission. She must have told him it was okay because he took a step closer. Amazing!

Goldilocks watched me. I took two tiny steps so I could stroke her coat. "You're sweet," I crooned. "Will you let me ride you?" It would help our chances of signaling a rescuer if I could train her, but for a moment I wanted to forget survival and simply imagine myself on her back, galloping along the water's edge, then, just for the fun of it, prancing into the ocean.

I pictured it all. The water would splash up, cooling us. Little Guy would shake his mane, loving the new game. Goldilocks would high-step farther out, past her chest, past her shoulders. When she hit a drop off, she would swim. Oh, I sighed, the thrill of it all.

When the mare showed no nervousness, I plucked some especially tasty looking grass and held it out to her. She ate the grass and seemed to want more. Since they could get their own grass, she must want the companionship. Could she belong to the watcher? Maybe he'd trained her.

I stroked her flank. "I'm just going to lean against you," I cooed. "Don't worry." Her ears lowered, then returned to their normal position. "That's a good girl," I sang.

Did I dare actually try to sit on her back? If she let me get close to her, maybe I could tame her. I could try making reins out of rope and ride her around.

Goldilock's ears flickered, and I sensed she'd leave soon. This might be my only chance. I decided to go for it.

I took a deep breath, clutched her mane, and swung my leg over. Too late, I saw her pinned ears. She lowered her head and bucked. I held on to her mane, but when she bucked harder a second time, I flew off. I threw my hands out to catch myself. *Bam!* I landed. Pain. Hot pain. In my right wrist.

Sand pelted my face as Goldilocks and Little Guy tore off. I lay still, hoping that if I kept my eyes closed, I could turn back time. Then I wouldn't have to face the stupidity, the enormous stupidity of what I'd done.

Chapter Thirteen
A Scream

I sat up. Pain pulsed through my arm and wrist. *What if I'd broken something? Idiot!*

I got to my feet, but immediately felt dizzy. Holding my injured arm with my left hand so I wouldn't jar my wrist, I stumbled back to camp. No Mirra.

Tears burned my eyes as I sank onto the sand. A few minutes later, Mirra appeared carrying something in her jacket. "Guess what I got," she began, until she saw my face. "What happened?"

"I tried to ride the palomino. She bucked me off. My wrist," I sucked in a deep breath, "it might be broken."

"Oh, Annie." She set down whatever she was carrying and hurried over to study my puffy wrist.

I pressed my lips together against the pain. "I ... I think I'm going to need some sort of splint and a sling."

God must have thought I wasn't getting enough practice being patient because He gave me another lesson. It seemed to take forever to find a plastic jug in the litter pile and for Mirra to hack away at it with the broken knife until it was the right size. Once she tied it around my arm, I had a splint. Finally, Mirra used the extra shirt to design a sling. The pain made me nauseous and when Mirra mentioned food, for once I didn't feel hungry.

As Mirra built up the fire, she told me she'd stayed at the pond awhile because she'd been trying to catch a duck. "It was amazing." Mirra's eyes were huge. "I had netting ready and snuck up to her. I was about to throw the net when she flew."

"But you were close."

"Uh-huh. I took three of her four eggs. I left her one."

"So she'll keep laying?"

"It was more that I felt sorry for her and wanted her to have at least one."

Mirra's chatter helped distract me from the pain, but while we waited for the eggs to cook, it returned with a fury. "I feel so stupid," I admitted.

"Yeah, well, we all have our moments." Mirra tugged at her shirt as if it needed straightening. "Annie, I ... I want to apologize."

I turned toward her.

"I shouldn't have blamed you for the life raft floating away." She looked at her broken nails. "I'm the one at fault. For all of this. Convincing you to come out with me so I could see Ryan. Not checking the forecast. Taking the boat out when I didn't know what I was doing." She looked up at me. "Without you, I wouldn't be alive."

I squirmed, not sure what to say.

After a few moments, she continued in a chattier voice. "What should we name this place?"

I was glad to think about anything besides the pain. *Banana* or *Lifeboat Island?* Nah.

"Brittany's good at coming up with nicknames. If you want a laugh, ask her for the nicknames she gave her sixth-grade teachers."

Brittany. The old feeling of being cast away for Brittany returned with a vengeance. "Castaway Island," I said darkly. "How about that for a name?"

"Yeah," she said, eyeing me suspiciously. "Okay."

I couldn't tell by her tone if she knew what I'd been thinking or not. I stared into the fire's dying flames. "How many matches do we have left?"

"Two."

"With all the garbage that's washed up here," I said, trying to ignore my throbbing arm, "I wonder if we could find a lighter."

"I doubt it would still work."

"It's worth trying. If you boil some water for drinking, I could hunt around. And maybe you could set up another signal fire. It might make the difference between being rescued. My plan to train Goldilocks sure didn't work out."

"Oh, you were thinking you could ride her to start the signal fires faster?"

"Yeah, either that or go to wherever the rescuers were."

My rotten luck continued. Even though I found two lighters, neither worked.

My gaze constantly returned to the ocean. Mirra's mom and our dads had been here. Dad ... I'd been close enough to see him, close enough to call out and have him hear me. *Dad, try again. Find us soon, before we run out of matches and food.*

A wave of intense pain shot up from my wrist to my arm and made me so dizzy I sank to my knees. It throbbed until I worried about fainting. My vision blurred, then I blinked.

Sea Stallion. He stood on a dune looking regal, strong, and determined. I felt Mom's presence. *You can get through this.* I stood up. The pain was still there, but, shoulders back, I returned to camp.

Once there, I felt better. Mirra had rolled a second log near the fire. She handed me a cup of warm water and sat alongside me. As we sipped, Mirra said, "I've been thinking more about that duck. Maybe we could try to catch it tomorrow."

"I can't help much, but think of it. Roast duck."

"Does your wrist hurt a lot?"

I nodded. "It's throbbing."

Mirra stood and pointed west. "I thought I'd go look for food in that direction."

"I'll come too." Even though I only had one good arm, I felt my pocket. The sharp stick was still there.

Mirra grabbed the tin. While we walked toward the west end, I kept listening for the smallest sound. Was someone behind that cluster of bushes or that high dune?

The waves pounded harder at this end of the island and there wasn't any driftwood or litter. "Let's hike back toward the pond," Mirra said. "I bet we'll find more wild peas."

We found peas and a few strawberries too. They were shriveled up, but we ate them anyway.

With High Dune on our right, we passed near the terns' nesting grounds. I was about to search for eggs when an odd pile of driftwood caught my eye. I bent down, threw some of the sticks off, and held my good hand over the ashes. Warm!

Someone had tried to camouflage a fire-pit. I scanned the area, my chest tightening. "Mirra. Quick. Look at this."

Mirra dropped to her knees and held her hand close. "Why doesn't he show himself and help us?"

A chill shivered up my spine as I thought of answers to that question, none of them good.

Spooked, we quickly planned our egg gathering. I waved off the terns while Mirra snatched the eggs. As we hurried back to camp, we jumped at every sound.

By the time our fire was in sight, it was nearly dark. I felt wrung out and my wrist throbbed so much I could barely think straight. Robot-like, I said, "Let's build up the fire before we put these on." Mirra helped and set the tin of water on the burning wood. She was quiet even after the water boiled and we smelled the eggs cooking. "Are you worried about the footprint guy?" I finally asked.

Mirra's face flushed. "Yeah, but there's something else. I, uh, I had to use the rest of our matches."

I jerked to my feet. "What!"

"The fire went out, so I struck a match." She squirmed. "I had bits of bark ready, but I hadn't blocked it from the wind, and it ... it fizzled out. I got it started the next time, though."

"But now we're totally out of matches!" I shot her a look. She gave me an ask-me-if-I-care look back. I lashed out. "You still don't get it, do you? Without fire we eat raw clams and get sick drinking dirty water. This is life and death for us. Life and death!" I couldn't catch my breath, so I closed my eyes. Purple and red and black dots bounced in my head. My life was falling apart, sinking like a capsized boat.

When I opened my eyes, I used my one good hand and counted all Mirra's screw-ups.

1. She took her dad's boat out without asking or checking the weather.
2. She wasted the only flare cartridge.
3. She broke the knife.
4. She slept while rescuers called for us.
5. She used our last two matches.

Maybe tomorrow I'd be able to list how she'd helped in a few ways, but right now I hurt too much and there was too much to do. "We should probably have two fires going," I began, "one for a backup. But that's a lot of work. If we stick with just one, we'll have to take shifts and guard it through the night."

Mirra pressed her lips together. She might hate my bossiness, but someone had to take charge.

"You take the first shift," I continued. "I have to get some sleep. Tomorrow we better figure out a roof so rain doesn't drown it."

As tired as I was, my guilty feelings prevented me from falling asleep right away. If only I could sleep until rescue came, sleep until I was back home in my own bed, sleep until this nightmare was over.

It seemed like I'd barely been asleep when Mirra woke me.

"Fire's still going," she mumbled. "See you in the morning." She lay down.

I added another piece of wood to the fire and spread out Mom's jacket. I sat facing the fire and ocean. Those moving dark shapes, were they horses or the footprint-maker? I shook my head. No need to freak myself out. Think of something happy like night campfires with my family. Joey would beg Mom to tell ghost stories. He'd squirm and squeal and cover his ears at the scary parts, but then as soon as Mom was finished, he'd beg for another.

I switched to lying on my back so my arm could rest on my chest. I stared at the moon and stars. They seemed mysterious and more intense here than they had at home.

I took several long breaths and looked skyward. Was Mom up there in heaven? I tried to picture her in a shimmery, white robe surrounded by platters of fruit, mountains of hamburgers, and chocolate fountains. Mom, the dietician in life, didn't frown at the unhealthy desserts in my fantasy. Instead, she invited me to join her and we each filled a plate until food spilled over the edge.

Before we could take a bite though, a rainstorm let loose. Rain! I jerked to my feet. Thunder boomed. The fire!

"Mirra! Get up." I fed the dwindling fire small pieces of wood. Mirra crawled out of the tent.

"My jacket," Mirra said, grabbing it from the cooler. "We can hold it over the fire."

Mirra handed me one side, but I needed two working hands to hold up both ends. Raindrops fell harder now. "Mirra, untie my splint."

"But—"

"Hurry!"

Mirra dropped her jacket and untied the splint. My wrist was puffy and in firelight looked bluish-brown. I couldn't worry about that now. I gritted my teeth and held the second corner up.

"Are you okay?" Mirra asked.

If I answered, if I dared to admit to the pain, I worried I'd never get it together again. So I stayed silent. We held our roof until water puddled so heavily on top of the jacket we had to scoot it over and dump the rainwater in the sand. We did that three more times. Seconds before I was going to admit the pain was too much and I wanted to stop, the rain let up.

"Should be good now," Mirra said. She took her sooty jacket back, and I lowered my arms, groaning.

Mirra brought back small pieces of kindling from our stash inside the tent and carefully added them to the fragile fire. Then she examined the rub marks on my wrist. "Let's try wrapping something soft around your wrist so the bottle doesn't rub." She came back with the shirt she'd worn the day we left. In fire-glow, she carefully wrapped it around my swollen wrist, then redid the splint and sling.

"Thank you," I said. "You ... you've been a big, a huge help."

Mirra nodded.

The sun rose.

Day eight.

* * *

After a clam and oyster breakfast, which left us almost full, we worked on a crude structure of poles and canvas to protect the fire. Mirra stopped hammering with her sandal and said, "Do you hear that?"

"Rescuers?" I asked, adrenaline rushing through my body.

"No, something in the brush. Bigger than the sparrows."

I listened but heard nothing unusual. "You still have your sharp stick?"

Mirra nodded.

"Let's hope it's a rabbit, not the watcher." When I found two long poles, I brought them to camp for extra weapons. Around midday, as our tern eggs boiled, Mirra sharpened them into spears. We didn't hear any other unusual sounds, but I liked having the spears close.

Mirra peeled the first tern egg. "Ah!" she squealed.

I looked. A chick complete with feathers and bulging eyes! "Eww!" My stomach roiled, but I forced myself to say, "I'll try another one."

When I broke a second egg apart, the sight made me run for the bushes. I didn't think I had enough in my stomach to throw up, but I did.

How could a person tell if the eggs were about to hatch? I didn't want to break open a developed one ever again. When I returned to camp Mirra said, "Let's forget tern eggs and go check on the duck. She might have more eggs or, if we're really lucky, maybe we can catch her."

"I want to take a bath in the pond," I said. "If we stay within shouting distance, do you think you could go alone?"

"I guess."

"I'll hurry."

At the pond, I wriggled out of my T-shirt and jeans using only one hand. Not knowing if I could get my underwear back on again, I left it.

Once I slipped into the cool water, I swished my good arm back and forth to hopefully clean my boils. Feeling the tension ease, I tipped my head back, took a deep breath, and dunked my head underwater, hoping to clean my salt-stiff hair.

Pretending I had fragrant shampoo, I used my left hand to massage my scalp. I dunked again. Afterward, I examined my boils. The fresh water seemed to have helped them.

I let myself relax and daydream. I pictured entering a restaurant. A waitress brought me a tall glass of ice water and served me an enormous bowl of salad with crisp lettuce, tomato, cucumber, and French dressing. She cleared away the empty dishes and brought a heaping plate of spaghetti with meatballs. For dessert, a hot fudge sundae.

A scream in the distance made me freeze. Splashing sounds were followed by a second scream. Cut off abruptly. Drowning! Mirra was drowning!

No time! I ran like never before. *She can't swim! I have to save her!*

The duck pond was in my line of vision, and a silhouette took shape. A man? A man was carrying Mirra away!

PART TWO

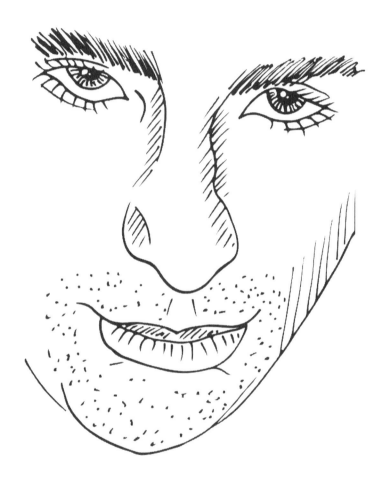

Chapter Fourteen
Roman

I ran in my drippy underwear yelling, "Mirra! Mirra!"

A guy with dark hair was carrying a dripping Mirra. He set her onto the ground, turning her on her side so she could cough out water. She sputtered, then sucked in air.

"Are you all right?" I pushed past the man and bent over her.

"Y-yes." She coughed, then brushed her wet hair out of her eyes.

I stared up into the dripping face of the guy who had saved Mirra's life.

Maybe a high school junior or senior with dark eyes and dark stubble. Green t-shirt, khaki shorts, and hiking boots. I tried to use my arms to shield my half-dressed body. "Who ... who are you?"

He looked back at Mirra. "Are you sure you're all right?"

She sat up. "Yes. Th-thank you. I was trying to catch that duck ... and slipped. I rolled into the water. A drop off." She sucked in air, then exhaled. "I can't swim."

The guy peeled off his wet T-shirt and offered it to me. "Want this?"

I took it. I struggled with my wrist to pull it over my head and over my wet underwear. It was only half on when he said, "Need help?"

"No!" I managed to slip it over my head, not caring how much my arm hurt. My embarrassment quickly turned to anger. "You're the person who's been hiding from us," I said. "You've been watching us the whole time. Who are you?"

"Roman. Roman Marshall," he said, his voice low and husky.

"Do you have a boat? Or a way to call for help?" Hope made my own voice higher than normal.

"No." Roman shook his head. "I'm sorry. I'm stuck here too."

I looked around. "Are you alone? How did you get here?"

Mirra shivered.

"Maybe we should go by your fire and take care of Mirra." Roman held out his hand and helped her to her feet.

He was telling me how to take care of Mirra, and he'd been spying on us. I ground my teeth. I walked behind them so Roman couldn't see me in the wet T-shirt and so I could study him from the back.

Mirra's steps were wobbly, but she said, "I'm okay. Really."

"How long have you been here?" I asked.

"Since the first of May."

It was hard to know if he'd been out in the sun since May or if his skin was naturally dark. His shorts, fraying at the hems, hung low on his hips, though, as if he'd been on the island diet for a while.

"Did you see us when we first landed?" I asked.

"Yes," he admitted.

We had nearly died, and he'd just watched. My nails dug into my palms. "You must have seen the rescue boat a few days ago. But you didn't call out to them. Why not?"

He hesitated, as if forming a lie.

I caught up to him and made my voice firm. "The truth, please."

"I'm sorry," he said, looking toward the ocean, "but I can't answer your questions."

Can't answer? Mirra and I looked at one another. "Can you at least tell us what kind of boat it was," I said, "or about the people on board?"

He hesitated, but eventually said, "Three people, red boat, about twenty-six feet."

Uncle Jim's boat. If he could see the red color, he must have been close. Rage, fear, and overwhelming sadness made me stumble along in silence. At camp, Mirra warmed herself at the fire. Remembering my lack of clothes, I murmured, "I'll be right back."

I walked away, but at the first clump of bushes, I ducked behind them and peered out. Roman was talking to Mirra. Was she in danger? Holding my aching wrist against my body, I jogged to the pond, got dressed as fast as I could, and jogged back. With every pounding step, I asked, *Why? He'd been close to rescuers but had stayed hidden. Why?*

Mirra held her hands out to the fire. She and I could be home now if this guy—Roman—had only called out. I stormed toward him, his T-shirt in my hand. I was sure, with my snarled hair, plastic bottle splint, and peeling skin, I looked like a wild animal. But before I reached him, I remembered he'd saved Mirra's life. I swallowed some of my snarl. "Can you at least tell us how far we are from the mainland?"

"I'd guess thirty miles," he answered. "Maybe more." He took his T-shirt back and glanced from me to Mirra. "So what happened to bring you here?"

He doesn't have answers, but asks us questions! When I didn't answer, Mirra did. "I took my dad's boat out. We were heading to an island to picnic." Her voice cracked. "A storm came up. We were ... we were washed overboard."

She didn't look like she could continue, so I did. "The boat sank. I inflated the life raft we had on board and we floated for three days before landing here."

"Wow," he said. "That must have been ... have been awful." A full minute passed before he turned to me. "And your arm?" His voice was gentle, but I wasn't about to be suckered in by him. Still, he might have helpful information.

"I sprained it falling off the Palomino mare. She was friendly, let me touch her, and put a rope in her mouth. But when I got on, she went ballistic. Have you been training her?"

"No, but I noticed she was friendly too."

My growly voice matched my stomach. "We're nearly starving. What have you been eating?"

"Mainly fish." His eyes took in our oyster and clam shells and stacked driftwood. "I can bring my fishing spear and seining net and we can try our luck."

Fresh fish. My stomach growled.

"Do you have matches?" Mirra asked hopefully.

"No, I ran out a few days ago. I've been banking my fire at night and so far it's stayed."

"Maybe you can show us," Mirra said. "Both the banking of the fire and how you catch fish."

"Sure. I'll get my net and come right back."

"Where's your camp?" Mirra asked.

"Not far." He made a vague sweep of his arm. I thought about asking to go with him, but I didn't want to leave Mirra.

I expected him to head toward where we'd found his fire, but he walked toward High Dune. As soon as he was out of earshot, Mirra clasped my good arm. "Do you think we can trust him?"

"We have to be on guard," I said, "but if he can teach us to bank our fire and catch fish, let's learn."

"I figure he can't be an awful person. He saved my life."

"Thank God because I never would have gotten to you in time." I paused. "If another boat comes, he might try to stop us from signaling." I pictured a boat motoring our way, Roman grabbing us, tying our hands with rope, using a piece of his T-shirt to gag us until the rescuers gave up and left. Two could play that game. "You and I should have rope and the knife in our pockets at all times. We might have to tie him up."

Mirra's raised eyebrows let me know that she knew it'd be hard to overpower him, but she accepted the piece of rope I gave her.

"He might be guarding something," I said.

"Like what?" Mirra asked.

"Something illegal. Maybe he and his partners hid it here. They left Roman behind to guard it, but they'll be back."

"I don't know..." Mirra said uncertainly. "He does look kinda like a bad boy—a hot bad boy for that matter—but he seems, I don't know, almost preppy."

I frowned. Mirra was right. He talked like a college kid. "Maybe he's part of some Outward Bound thing where he has to try to survive on his own."

"Why not tell us that then?"

"I don't know," I mumbled.

Mirra pulled dry clothes out of the cooler and headed for the tent. When she returned, I noticed she'd knotted her dad's shirt at her waist, emphasizing her figure. She hung her wet clothes over bushes and turned to me. "You sure were funny standing there in his T-shirt spouting off questions."

I blushed, remembering.

My eyes swept the island, stopping at High Dune. Could he be hiding drugs? Maybe in a metal box? I pictured finding it, breaking open its rusty lock, and pulling out bags of white powder. I blinked, wishing the scene away. All I knew is that he had the means to catch fresh fish, and I intended to learn all I could about surviving on this island.

Mirra finger-combed her hair. I turned away, disgusted. Typical Mirra, wanting to look good for a boy, even one who could be trouble.

Roman's shelter couldn't have been too far away because it only took him about fifteen minutes to come back. He carried a net and a sharpened pole.

Mirra hurried toward him. "I don't know why we didn't think of netting or spearing fish." She gave me a look I translated as, *How stupid you were, Annie, not to think of this.* "Which is best, Roman, the pond or the lake?"

Which is best, Roman? I mimicked her fan girl tone in my head.

"The pond with the ducks seems to have more fish," he said. "Will it bother you to hang out there?"

"I'll be okay if it's shallow." Mirra coyly smiled at Roman.

Tell me she isn't flirting even now.

Mirra trotted alongside Roman. He asked, "Were you able to get a hold of the Coast Guard before you sank?"

"No."

His shoulders seemed to relax.

"The radio died before we could," Mirra continued. "Our families have no idea where we are."

"Where are you from?" Roman's voice sounded strained, and he spoke quickly.

"Friendly, Maine," Mirra said. "You?"

"Just north of Portland. Portland, Maine, that is."

"How old are you?" Mirra asked.

"Eighteen." Roman pulled up his low-riding shorts.

"We're fourteen," Mirra said. "I'm almost fifteen. We'll start high school this fall. That is, if we—well, you know."

Roman remained silent.

I blinked, trying to process all of this. They were talking like they met at the mall, not here on a remote island. I came up alongside Roman, every sense on high alert. "I have some questions," I began in a determined voice. "What are you using for a shelter?"

He hesitated, but then finally answered. "I found some poles on shore and made a kind of tepee. It's in a valley between those two dunes." He pointed toward the east end.

"Aw," I said, "in Green Valley."

"Annie likes to name things," Mirra explained. "She'll have names for the litter piles next."

I wasn't going to let her comment make me mad. Roman might be able to answer a question that had been bugging me. "A lot of stuff gets washed up here. Do you know why?"

"It's the currents bringing it in," Roman started to explain as we neared the pond.

The duck quacked and flew from her nest. "I'll get you one of these days," Mirra said to it. "Yum. Roasted duck."

Roman stared into the pond water. "So the secret to spearing fish is to aim where the fish isn't."

"Huh?" Mirra said it, but I was confused too.

"Because of light refraction."

Mirra shot me a look that said drug runners don't talk like this.

I struggled to remember a science lab where we set a pencil in a cup of water, and the pencil looked bent. The teacher had used the word refraction then.

"Aim below the fish and go for piercing it in the side. Annie, do you want to try the spear and Mirra and I can work the net?"

"Sure." I stood in water up to his waist, grabbed the spear with my good hand, held my arm in the ready position, and concentrated on the water.

Roman unwound the seining net he had tied to two poles.

"If you get back to Maine," Mirra prompted, "you'll be able to make up your schoolwork and graduate, right? The school wouldn't dare hold being stranded on an island against you." She took the pole which Roman handed to her. "Will you go to college?"

"Not sure." Roman had unrolled the net and he now held the other pole. "Stand here in the shallow and keep the net low. I'm going to sweep and together we'll drag the net."

I still hadn't seen a fish and wished I'd been part of the seining team. Then I did see a flash. I thrust the spear. Missed.

"Did you get it?" Roman asked, still working the net toward shore.

"No." I'd forgotten to aim below the fish and I hadn't gone for its side.

"If that jarring hurts your wrist," Roman said, "you and Mirra could switch."

Roman talked like he cared, but he wasn't fooling me. He had to be mad that Mirra's near-drowning made him blow his cover.

"I'll keep trying," I answered, my voice without emotion.

I kept watching Mirra and Roman and although I did see two more fish, I missed both of them.

Roman and Mirra were halfway through their third pass when Mirra cried, "We got a whopper!" When they brought the net up to shore, they had a fish the size of Roman's outstretched hand and another twice that size. Altogether they'd gotten five fish.

Mirra giggled. "Let's get these on the fire."

I pushed aside any bad feelings about my misses. We had food to fill our bellies.

Roman carried the net and the fish. When we got back to camp, I was about to add fuel to the fire when Roman held up his hand.

"Not yet," he said. "These embers are perfect."

I set down the wood. "I've done some camping, but we never baked fish."

"You have a knife, right?" Roman's brows hid his eyes. The spy knew we did. "I lost mine in the ocean. I only have an ax. Not too good for cleaning fish."

I hesitated. Roman and Mirra both noticed. Mirra's face reddened and Roman shifted uncomfortably. I reached in my pocket and handed Roman the knife.

The light was dim, and I had to stand right next to Roman to study how he cleaned the fish. I'd never enjoyed fishing and the few times I'd gone, Dad and Steven had always done the cleaning. I paid attention now. Using the small log as a table to slice into the fish's belly, Roman pulled out the guts, cut off the head and tail and then laid the meat on the embers. The second fish was nearly the same size. "What kind of fish are these?" I asked.

"No idea. I wish I knew more about fish."

And I wish I knew more about you. If another rescue boat comes, will you help us signal? Or will you do whatever it takes to make sure they don't find us?

Chapter Fifteen
"Kill it!"

The air turned cooler and Mirra warmed her hands over the fire. I stood as close to the baking fish as possible. "We've had to stand guard over the fire to make sure it doesn't go out," I told Roman.

Mirra told Roman how we'd hauled the cooler into the little boat. She showed him our supplies, including the green cups. "We can use these for dishes," he said. "I'll divide them up." Soon the smell of the roasted fish wafted toward me.

Roman used green twigs to pull the fish out of the fire. He gave Mirra and me the biggest pieces.

"*Voilá!*" Mirra said. "Dinner is served."

"*Voilá?*" I asked.

"Hello, Annie, don't you know what that means?" She rolled her eyes at Roman as if to say, *I'm so sorry about my lame friend.*

I wanted to roll my eyes at how hard Mirra was trying to impress him, but I held back. After all, I'd slipped up and made her feel stupid when I'd snorted about her dumb *I-didn't-know-dragons-were-real* comment. I had to let this go so I could concentrate on the great-smelling fish. I blew on it and peeled back the skin. Mmm, moist and flaky. I brought a piece to my mouth and savored it before swallowing. I licked my fingers and picked up a second piece. Delicious.

As the sun set, Mirra told Roman the story of how we'd ended up here. He asked a few questions but didn't bother to tell us a single thing about himself. He stood up. "I better let you two get some sleep." He picked up our cups, walked far from camp to throw out the bones, and returned and rinsed them out with a little water.

"Will you come by tomorrow?" Mirra asked, playing with her hair.

"Sure. Maybe we can try for the duck."

"That'd be great." I heard the smile in Mirra's voice and ground my teeth.

I faced Roman and tried to keep my voice even. "We have signal fires set up ready to be lit if another boat comes."

Roman nodded. "I know. I've seen them. Oh, that reminds me. Do you want me to bank your fire?"

"Yes," Mirra answered, still star-struck. "That'd be great. Then we won't have to stay up all night to guard it."

I watched closely as Roman sprinkled a layer of sand on the top. "It's still smoldering under there," he said, "but it won't use as much fuel. In the morning, stir it around, add wood, and it should be roaring in no time."

"Thanks," Mirra said. "And if something would happen to it, we'll still have yours!" She beamed.

He nodded. "Hey, would it be all right if I borrow your knife tonight? I'll be careful with it and bring it back bright and early."

Taking our only knife? And for what?

"Annie has it," Mirra said.

He looked at me and when I still hesitated, he said, "Before I lost mine, I'd been carving a calendar pole. I'd like to catch it up. Also, I could try sharpening it with my ax blade."

Sharpen it so you can hold it to our throats?

Still, the knife did need sharpening. And for that matter, if he was going to kill us, he could use his ax. Not wanting to picture that grisly scene, I stood up quickly and handed him the knife.

He vanished into the night.

"I hope giving him our knife wasn't a mistake." I rubbed my forehead.

"Seriously? The guy's been helping us and he saved me from drowning. He's not going to kill us." Mirra clicked her tongue as if to say *you're such an idiot.*

"Don't you see," I began, my voice low and fierce, "that by letting the rescue boat leave, he probably already has."

* * *

The next morning, Mirra crawled out of the tent first. She French-braided her hair while I brushed my teeth. She and I had made twig toothbrushes a week or so ago. I walked over to the fire and awkwardly stirred the banked embers. My sprained wrist, useless in its sling, ached worse than ever. But I forgot all worries as a flicker appeared, then a small flame that grew into a bright fire. "It worked!"

A *whooshing* sound made me look toward a tall patch of grass. I'd heard a similar sound shortly after we arrived. Roman's head appeared above the grasses. It must have been him. It still annoyed me that we'd been nearly dead from starvation and he hadn't helped.

"How are you doing?" he asked.

"Good," Mirra answered. "Banking the fire worked great." She pointed to the spear, net, and ax he carried. "Were you a boy scout or a hunter?" When he didn't answer, she kept on. "Is that a wallet in your pocket? Why do you carry it around?"

"It makes me feel, well, normal."

"I get that," Mirra said. "I got up and French-braided my hair right away as if it was a regular day."

Roman handed me the knife. "It might be a bit sharper so be careful."

I will be careful, I silently answered. *Of you.*

Mirra carried the driftwood inside the tent. Left alone, I watched Roman warily, feeling like a seal not knowing whether a shark swam nearby.

He finally broke the silence. "How's your arm doing?"

I held up the splint. "It hurts."

"Let me see." He gently untied the splint, winced at my wrist's puffiness, and retied it without comment.

I tucked my arm back to my side.

"I wish ... " Roman began, but his words trailed off to nothingness.

"You wish what?" I tried to keep my voice neutral.

"I wish we could turn back time and get do-overs."

"Do-overs would be great."

Mirra returned from the tent. She looked from Roman to me, raising her eyebrows. When neither of us explained, she said, "The net's full again."

"The net?" Roman asked.

"Annie tied a piece of net near the roof of our tent. We keep driftwood inside so it stays dry."

He gave me an approving nod.

"So are we trying for the duck today?" Mirra asked.

"I think we should," Roman said. "Once we get it roasting on the fire, we can work on breakfast."

It made more sense to get breakfast started first; maybe have fish baking while we tried to catch the duck. But Roman seemed to have taken charge. My jaw muscles tightened.

"So what's the plan?" Mirra asked.

"With Annie's wrist hurting," Roman said, "you and I should do the netting and Annie can scare it toward us."

I wasn't sure how I felt about Roman calling the shots, but answered, "I can be pretty scary."

Roman gave me a half smile. "We should carry the small log in case we need a chopping block."

When Roman left to get the log, Mirra squeezed my good arm. "I'll keep asking questions. I'll get him to talk."

I gave her an encouraging nod.

Mirra grabbed the cookie tin, and we set off. She made her stride match Roman's and even took a turn carrying the ax. We had the pond in sight when she finally said, "That fish we had yesterday was delicious." She cleared her throat. "Are you good at hunting too?"

"My dad took me out a few times, but I didn't love it."

"Does your dad know you're okay?" Mirra asked.

Instead of answering, Roman set down the small log and ax. "I see something moving in the cattails. If we get it, Mirra, you should kill it. With Annie's wrist and my not always being around, you might have to take over."

His not being around? Did he mean he might be on another part of the island, or did he know he'd be gone soon? He rubbed the back of his neck and shook his head slightly, almost as if telling himself, *I can't care about these girls. Not when I know what I'll have to do to them.*

"Like cut its head off?" Mirra said. "Me?"

"Yes. Can you do it?"

Her voice sounded surprisingly strong when she said, "I can try."

"Good," Roman whispered. "Stand in the shallow end. Throw the net over it if it comes your way. Annie, you're the troubleshooter, okay?"

Mirra and I nodded. As we got nearer, the duck eyed us suspiciously. I crept closer. She lifted her wings to take flight. A millisecond later, Roman launched his net. *Whizzz.* It covered the duck, but her flapping wings threw the net off. She was escaping when I charged her, waving my good arm and steering her toward Mirra. Mirra's net trapped the duck's wings for only a second, but it was long enough.

Mirra pinned the duck's wings, pressed its body against her chest, and ran. Roman helped pin it down on the chopping block.

Mirra raised the ax, hesitated a moment, then brought the ax down. *Whoosh, thud.* She'd cut the head clean off.

As the blood oozed out of the neck, I raised my good hand in a high-five. "Well done," I said. Was this really the same girl who'd closed her eyes during violent movie scenes and hated the thought of carrying a weapon? I stared at this new Mirra with her smudged chin and glowing cheeks.

Roman's face was slick with sweat. He turned to us. "Come on, gang. Let's get this sucker plucked."

Soon, we had feathers floating in the air, in our hair, and on our clothes. Roman used the knife and his long thumbnail to get the stubborn ones.

"Do you want to gut it?" Roman asked Mirra, offering her the knife.

"How about if I watch," Mirra said. "Maybe I'll try next time." She leaned in for a good look.

"I hate to admit this," Roman said, "but I get squeamish. I never made it through gutting a deer, but maybe I can handle this." With the duck on the chopping block, Roman sliced its belly.

I breathed in through my mouth so I wouldn't have to smell the gore. Roman held his breath and quickly pulled out the guts. He dug through the tangled parts and once he held up some pieces, he let out his breath. "Heart, liver, and gizzard. Ought to be full of nutrients."

"I'll boil them up once we're back at camp." I studied the gizzard, thinking back to watching Dad clean a turkey. "Don't we need to slice the gizzard open and, I don't know, clean it?"

"Ah, maybe." Roman sliced it open and scraped out some sandy stuff. "Yep. Good call, Annie. Let's bring everything to the pond so we can wash it off."

It was late morning when we finally arrived back at camp. "Storm's coming in," Roman commented, sniffing the air.

The wind had picked up.

"Looks like rain," Mirra said. "Can we get this cooked in time?"

"Let's get the fire ready," I said. With Mirra's help, I repositioned the roof over the fire and added wood. By the time Roman had the duck ready, the thunderstorm had rolled in.

"I'd better check my fire," Roman called.

He'd just left for his shelter when the storm let loose. Mirra and I scooted into the flapping tent. "We should have cleaned the duck and let him take care of his fire," I said. "We could lose both fires."

Mirra shivered.

The rain and wind whipped at the tent for half an hour or more. Then the storm stopped. Mirra and I stepped out. The canvas roof over the fire had held.

After we tended the fire, I said, "Let's get sticks to make a spit." I thought back to a Beetle-eater episode. "We'll need something we can stick through the duck and then hang it over the hot embers."

She eyed the sticks we'd brought back for weapons, pulled at her jeans which were no longer skintight, and said, "Yeah, but let's hurry. I'm starved."

While searching, I told her about the show where Beetle-eater had roasted a rabbit. I soon found two Y-shaped pieces of driftwood and Mirra picked up a straight skewer stick. Back at camp, Mirra used the knife to sharpen the ends of the Y-sticks. She pushed them into the sand. "The tricky part's getting it the right distance from the fire," I said, adjusting it so the meat would cook but not burn.

The clouds had cleared by the time we'd positioned the duck on the spit. "In a few hours, we'll have a feast!" Mirra said. "I'm going to bring over the cooler for a table."

I looked for Roman. No sign of him.

Mirra nearly skipped to the cooler. Carrying the bulky thing toward the fire, she stumbled over a piece of driftwood. Time switched to slow motion as the cooler slipped out of her hands, falling toward the roof supports. It hit the poles causing the canvas to drop onto the fire collapsing the duck spit and smothering the flames.

"Mirra!" I cried. I fumbled to lift the canvas with one hand. Mirra stood frozen. "Help me!"

Together, we threw off the canvas and lifted the duck out of the mess. I dropped to my knees and stirred the smothered embers. "Dry bark!" I cried.

Mirra ran for the tent, returning seconds later with two handfuls. She threw them on the dying fire.

Another cloud burst. Rain fell as hard and sudden as before. "Grab the roof!" Ignoring the hot pain in my arm, I held half of the canvas. Mirra's hands clutched the other.

Roman jogged toward us. He blew on the wet ashes. Nothing. He kept trying, but before long, I knew it was useless.

Roman groaned. He stood up. "My fire's out too."

What's the use? I might as well give up. Curl up on the sand, fall asleep, and stay there.

A horse whinnied in the distance. Sea Stallion? It whinnied again.

I felt Mom's presence stronger than ever. *No, Mom,* I silently said. *I won't give up. Someday I'll get back to Dad, Steven, and Joey. Someday I'll return home.*

Chapter Sixteen
Plans

Mirra, Roman, and I stared at the raw, drippy duck in silence.

The rain eased up, but a stiff wind blew in from the north, making me shiver and wonder how soon summer would turn into autumn and then to winter.

My stomach growled. I looked at the soggy duck. "Do we dare eat it raw?"

"I worry about parasites." Roman ran his hands through his wet hair. "If only we had something like a magnifying lens that could bring the sunlight to a focal point and start a fire."

"Hey!" Mirra's eyes grew wide. "I just thought of something. I don't know if it would work, but my father left a water bottle in our boat once and it burned the seat cushion."

"It was filled with water?" Roman asked.

"Uh huh."

He shrugged. "It's worth a try."

Rather than use our two clean water bottles, we hiked to the biggest debris pile, dug around, finally found two, and filled them with ocean water. "Does it matter if the water is cold?" Mirra asked.

"We wouldn't want condensation to be on the outside," Roman said, "but by the time we get to camp, it should be good. Keep your eye out for dark-colored tinder."

It took a while, but we found some dry bark that was brown. "Let me have one of the bottles," I said. "This is something I can do."

"Mirra," Roman asked, "do you want to hold the other or get us some cattail heads?"

"I'll try the bottle."

Mirra and I experimented holding our bottles in different positions. The sunlight streamed through. We got pinpricks of light to fall on the bark, but we were far from getting a flame. The wind was picking up and clouds were building in the west. We had to hurry.

When Roman returned, he pulled out his brown wallet. "Just thought of this." He handed Mirra and I a one-dollar bill. "Great tinder." He quickly returned his wallet to his pocket.

It suddenly hit me that Roman might have lied about carrying his wallet around to "feel normal." He might be afraid we'd sneak into this shelter and look through it.

As Roman dug out the inside, dry cattail fluff and sprinkled it around the bark to feed any sparks we might get, I plotted. We kept holding the bottle without any luck.

"Be right back," Roman said. "Nature calls."

Once out of Roman's hearing, I said, "I'd love to have a chunk of time to look inside that wallet. We could find out if he'd given us his real name and look through his cards and pictures. Any ideas how we can get it?"

Mirra raised her eyebrows. "Steal it when he's naked in the pond?"

I laughed, jiggling the bottle. I held it steady again.

Roman was already strolling back.

"Is that smoke?" Mirra said a few minutes later. "I think I'm getting smoke!"

"Yes!" I echoed. "Me, too!" I added cattail fluff and bits of the dollar bill. I got a flame! Adrenaline shot through me. *Go fire, go!*

"Yoo-hoo!" Mirra exclaimed.

Poof! The cattail fluff was really burning now.

Within a few minutes, we had our camp fire going again. "Let's celebrate tonight," Mirra said.

"First," Roman said, "let me take a burning stick and start my fire as a backup. Are you okay restarting the duck?"

"Let's do it together," Mirra said. "We'll walk with you. I can carry some embers in case the stick goes out."

My eyes caught hers. Brilliant, I communicated.

"O-kay." Roman's long hair covered his eyes, but I guessed he wasn't happy about us seeing his shelter.

After the duck was roasting on a spit, Roman grabbed a red-hot stick, and I helped Mirra put some hot embers in the tin. Using her dad's shirt for a hot pad, Mirra carried the tin. We headed east. I kept looking back to check on the fire.

We passed the lake and arrived at Green Valley. Roman's shelter, set in a dip between two grassy dunes, was well hidden.

Roman had taken a bunch of poles and sticks and formed a tepee shape. The doorway was so big and the spaces between the supports so wide, I asked, "Doesn't the sand whip in?"

"I throw the raft over it if it's windy or rainy." Roman pointed to a deflated raft a distance away. It was blue, so it wasn't our raft, but strange that he'd never mentioned it before.

"Did you use that to get from your boat to shore?" Mirra asked.

"Uh-huh." He fed the flicker until it built to a flame. "It's wrecked. I, uh, kept it too close to the fire. Burned holes in it."

What excuse could I make to check it out?

"So," I began, "you've never told us exactly what happened to your boat."

"I decided, spur of the moment, to go for a ride." He added another piece of wood to the fire.

Liar, I wanted to say, but his mouth opened to say more.

"No one knew I was taking off, and they don't have a clue what direction I went."

You wanted it that way, I silently added.

"The weather turned nasty like it did for you," he concluded.

"You jump in your boat and take off because you feel like it?" I asked.

"Hey, I'm an impetuous guy." He tried a charming grin. "Come on, this fire's looking good. Let's head back to our duck."

I didn't move.

"First," Mirra said, "I've been, uh, trying to figure out how many days Annie and I have been here. Did you keep track on your calendar pole?"

"Let me check." He quickly ducked inside, making it clear he didn't want us following him.

I hurried over to the raft. No burn marks. Not even any holes. He'd lied, which would justify us stealing this if we were ever desperate enough to attempt rafting to another island or trying for the mainland.

Roman scooted out of his shelter without the calendar pole. His eyes narrowed to see me walking away from the raft. "Nine days," he told Mirra, his voice as frosty as the night wind. "You ready?"

I was ready all right. First chance I got, I intended to see if the raft held air.

As the three of us headed in the fading light toward the roasting duck, Mirra smiled coyly at Roman. "So you and your girlfriend are out boating," she said, "and she gets mad. Dumps you off in a flimsy raft and takes off. You must have really ticked her off." Mirra's tone might have been teasing, but her narrowed eyes meant she was gauging Roman's reaction.

"It wasn't like that." He gave her a *quit-prying* look.

I wanted to know what happened to Roman's boat. The question hung in the air as darkness crept in. Even from this distance, I saw that our cooking fire blazed brightly. Too brightly. We ran toward it.

"It's the grease from the duck," Roman said.

I cringed to see the scorched skin.

"In some restaurants," Mirra said, her voice happy but forced, "you have to pay extra for blackened meals."

Roman smiled at her. "Let's check if the insides are done."

"Let me wash this out first," Mirra said, grabbing the cookie tin. After Mirra swished water in the tin, Roman carried the spit with the duck over to it. He used the knife to cut the duck into pieces, wiped the blade clean with his T-shirt, then handed the closed knife to me.

The dark meat was chewy and not quite done in spots, but other parts were so flavorful I licked the grease from around my mouth. When I saw Mirra sucking on a bone, I grinned. Yes, unanswered questions nagged at us, but for once, our stomachs were full.

As soon as we finished eating, Roman said goodnight and took off for his shelter. I lay awake trying to figure him out. Had he lied about the burn marks on the raft so we wouldn't take it and try to get away? Why would he care unless he intended to use it for himself? If he was here guarding drugs, why didn't he have survival things like water, matches, food, and a tent? Was he keeping a calendar pole so he knew when his partners would pick him up? Would it be soon? My brain was on overload, and it took a long time to fall sleep.

Partners, I dreamed. *A man with a full black beard, holster low on his hips. A woman, hardened, looking desperate. They pull their dinghy onto our shore.*

"Quick!" I whisper to Mirra. "They can't know we're here. Scatter the woodpile." While she works at that, I rip down our tent and scatter the canvas, poles, and ropes. "Hide!" I grab a branch and walk backwards, trying to cover our tracks. Once we're on harder, grassy ground, I drop the branch and we run to hide in a clump of bushes.

Blackbeard calls, "Roman!"

The woman says, "Strange. I see more than one set of footprints."

Blackbeard calls for Roman again. When no one answers, the man laughs and says, "Not like he can run anywhere."

Blackbeard spots Sea Stallion. He pulls out a pistol. "Watch me hit that white moon on his forehead."

Blackbeard raises his pistol, aiming at Sea Stallion. I jump up to distract him. Blackbeard swings the pistol toward me.

Boom!

I jerked to a sitting position in the tent, hitting my head on something hard. The drying wood in the net that hung under the ceiling. I rubbed my scalp.

"Annie?" Mirra mumbled.

"I'm okay, just a bad dream." I tried to clear my head.

The musty, canvas smell from the tent made it hard to breathe. I rearranged my life jacket pillow and tried to lie on a patch of skin without bites or boils. I finally settled onto my back. Think of something pleasant, I told myself.

I pictured myself walking along the beach with Mom, Dad, and my brothers. Mom asks me what I want for dinner. "Mac and cheese," I tell her. "And a big salad, watermelon, and apple pie with ice cream for dessert."

She laughs. "Sounds delicious. Let's head back and start the pie first. We'll make it together."

I slept until the chilly morning air crept in. I wanted to keep thinking about Mom, but Mirra stirred. "You awake?" she asked.

"Uh-huh."

Her voice was light and teasing. "I know how I can get Roman out of his pants."

I blinked.

Mirra laughed. "I'm talking about getting his wallet. Now, here's the plan..."

Chapter Seventeen
Exposed

R oman walked toward where Mirra and I stood feeding the fire. "Good morning," he called.

"Good morning." Mirra picked up the piece of rope she'd set near the sitting log and threaded it through the belt loops of her mom's shorts. "I wore these in case I could talk you into giving me a swimming lesson. I'd like to learn in case I fall in again, and with Annie's broken wrist, it'd be hard for her to teach me."

Roman lifted his eyebrows. Mirra's detailed explanation would make anyone suspicious. Instead of answering, Roman picked up a large piece of driftwood and broke it into tinder pieces.

Mirra had tied her rope belt, but the shorts still rode low on her hips. A memory of our spring Career Day last year flashed before me. Mirra's mom had brought in Hawaiian music, and she and Mirra had demonstrated the hula. Mirra had worn a grass skirt, but it kept falling down showing her short-shorts. "This thing is huge on me," she'd said. The boys, mesmerized, hadn't cared. At the time, I'd looked at her model-thin waist and vowed to go on a strict diet. How stupid I'd been. I'd never be tiny like her.

"So what do you think about a swimming lesson today?" Mirra asked again.

"Sure," Roman answered, making me wonder if Mirra had charmed him too. "Let's do it later, after it warms up a little."

Mirra stared off in space. Since she'd nearly drowned in the duck pond, she must be super scared. Yet she was going through with it.

Around midday, Mirra asked, "Can we have the lesson in Duck Pond?"

"It's weedier than the lake," Roman said.

"That's okay." She shot me a look. "It's warmer."

It also had better cover, so I'd be able to sneak up and grab his wallet.

When they headed out, I lagged behind, bringing the tin. If Roman saw me lurking, I could say I was gathering wild peas or hauling water.

"So," I overheard him ask Mirra, "have you ever had lessons?"

"Uh-huh. When I was a kid. Mom brought Annie along, probably so I'd try harder, but I threw a hissy fit and spent most of my time just dangling my feet. Mom finally let me quit. Now, though, I'm motivated. If we ever get back home..." It took her a long time before she could continue. "I'd like to visit my grandma in Hawaii. Maybe try surfing there. So I'd better learn to swim."

Mirra was skilled at this. Even I couldn't tell if this was the truth or a lie.

"Hawaii," Roman said, his voice light for once. "Gnarly, dude. Hang ten."

"Ha! Have you ever been to Hawaii?"

"Twice. Snorkeled Hanauma Bay, hiked to Kilauea at night to watch the lava flow, rode a helicopter next to a waterfall."

Annie nodded. She'd suspected Roman came from money. Here was proof.

"My grandparents live in Napali." Mirra flicked her hair. "I might apply to the University of Hawaii. I've only been to the islands once, when I was seven."

"Are you a native Hawaiian?"

"Half." Mirra looked up at him. "How about you?"

"Italian and Greek."

"So, tell me about your family, your parents."

He gave her a sideways glance. "You're just stalling. It's time to get wet."

I caught a slight hesitation, but she was soon in the water up to her knees. Roman pulled out his wallet, laying it by the edge of the pond. I wished the grass in that area wasn't so thin, but at least his back was toward me.

Quietly, I set the cookie tin down and casually walked nearby.

"The first thing we'll do," Roman said, "is walk out deep so you can get used to putting your face in the water."

With Roman's back turned, I quickly ducked down, crawling through the grass as best I could with my splinted arm. Once the grass thinned out and I neared the wallet, I waited for my chance. When Mirra called, "No, no, don't let go," I reached out, exposing my arm and chest, and grabbed the wallet. Quick! Scoot back into the grass.

As Roman calmly said, "You're all right. I won't let you go under," I looked at his license. He hadn't lied about his age, but his real last name was Macchio, not Marshall.

I shuffled through cards and photos until I landed on a picture of Roman with his arm around a gorgeous girl with dark hair nearly to her waist. The next photo, of her face, showed bright eyes and a friendly smile. I flipped it over. The pen marks were faded, but I made out two words: "Love you, Tamara."

"You're doing good," Roman declared, reminding me I needed to hurry. "Should we quit for now? Or do you want to try putting your face in the water and doing a few strokes?"

"Couple more minutes," Mirra said, her voice trembling only slightly.

I rifled through the credit cards. An airline card said *Elite status*. Other cards said *Gold Member* or *Preferred Customer*.

While they continued the lesson, I slipped the wallet back in place. Oh no! My tracks. Just like last night's Blackbeard nightmare. I grabbed a twig, crawled backward, and tried to erase them. There. He might not notice. I kept low until I hit the tall grass, then I scooted away.

I hurried until I was nearly back to camp.

I had tea brewed by the time I heard Roman and Mirra's approaching chatter. They were talking about Hawaii again. While Roman began adjusting the lean -to protecting the fire, Mirra rummaged through the cooler. "I'm going to rinse out my clothes," she called.

"I'll come along," I said.

As soon as we were out of earshot, Mirra spun around. "Did you do it?"

I nodded. "He gave us a fake last name making me think he's been on the news. Does Macchio ring a bell?"

"No, but you know me. I never listen to the news."

"I don't recognize it either. His wallet's full of twenties, credit cards, and pictures." I told her about Tamara.

"Hmm, I'm not surprised he has a girlfriend. Wonder why he never talks about her or his family? The elite cards don't surprise me either. All the travel he talks about and those hiking boots of his weren't cheap." She plunged her mom's shorts into the water.

I swished my T-shirt with one hand and Mirra squeezed out the water for me. While she did, I tried to figure out why a good looking, rich teenager would want to hide out on a deserted—or nearly deserted— island. My clothes might be a little brighter, but I wasn't any closer to an answer.

The sun was low in the sky by the time we'd roasted clams and boiled the duck liver, heart, and gizzard for dinner. We filled our cups and sat around the fire.

"So," Mirra said, "I have a fun idea. It's a version of Truth-or-Dare."

I felt my neck muscles tighten, thinking of Brittany and the other girls she'd left me for. Amazing after all I'd been through these past days that her betrayal could still hurt this much.

"It's called *Deep Secrets*," Mirra continued. "We can start by telling something we normally wouldn't tell."

I immediately thought of the dark secret about Mom's death that I hadn't told anyone, especially not Dad. I wasn't ready to voice what I'd done.

"I don't—" Roman began, but Mirra cut him off.

"I'll start. Let's see. My confession is a bit gross. It's that, uh, since being here, my pee smells funny. Kind of like nail polish remover."

"Hey," I said, glad to have moved on to a humorous topic. "Mine does too."

"I'm guessing we're not getting enough fruits and vegetables," Roman said.

"Oh, good, now I feel better. I think." Mirra smiled at Roman, then turned to me. "Your turn."

I knew why Mirra was doing this, but like Roman, I wasn't keen on playing. *Secret* seemed to be my middle name. My mind flipped from the one I kept about Mom's death to something so embarrassing I blushed.

"Whoa." Mirra sat forward. "Must be a good one."

Although I'd prefer not saying, telling this secret would be better than telling the other one. "It's just that," I began, "I'd been writing in a diary. I kept it in my secret box. Dad might have found it."

"So what is it you're most worried about him reading?" Mirra asked.

"I shouldn't have to say." The slight tilt of Mirra's head toward Roman reminded me we'd never get Roman to tell anything revealing if we didn't too. "Okay, I wrote about being scared."

"Of what?" Mirra asked.

I stole a look at Roman. Big mistake. My cheeks flamed. What could I say instead of *guys and dating*?

"Growing up." My answer sounded like the title of one of those pamphlets the health teacher gave us in fourth grade, and Mirra picked up on it.

"Annie. You're supposed to tell the truth. Was it about Nick?" Mirra turned to Roman. "Annie has a crush on this track star." Now she looked back at me. "You sit together on the bus, sometimes, don't you?"

Mirra would know that answer if she hadn't started riding with Brittany's dad every day. I shrugged. "We sat together once."

"Ha!" Mirra laughed. "That's hysterical."

I glared at her. Hysterical because she doesn't think a boy could like me?

"Don't get mad," Mirra said. "It's just that you're so brave in some things." She turned to Roman. "Annie slashed a shark that was circling our lifeboat right in the eye, but," back to me, "you're scared of guys."

I tilted my head and raised my eyebrows. Mirra knew me well.

"Hey," Roman said, "Girls should be cautious."

Mirra and I glanced at each other. What did that mean?

Mirra gave me an encouraging smile. "Anything else hidden in this secret box?"

My face flamed again as I realized if I didn't return, Dad would eventually open that box.

"Okay," Mirra said, half-laughing. "Leave it to our imagination. We'll move on to Roman."

"Well, I never admit this, but I like gardening, flowers especially." He raised his eyebrows. "I don't exactly share this with my buddies."

Mirra's face revealed disappointment, but then she laughed. "We'll remember that when we meet them."

I finished my piece of liver. "These organ meats aren't too bad and are probably full of vitamins we need. I wish I knew more about seaweed and whether all of it is safe to eat."

"I miss not being able to Google stuff like that," Roman said. He took a small piece of gizzard and heart. "Here's to improving the smell of our pee."

I smiled, feeling almost normal.

I hated to see that last bit of duck disappear. I wondered when the ducks would start migrating. Even though it was mid-summer, should we be planning for colder weather?

"Let's take a walk before dark," Mirra suggested.

We added wood to the fire and set off toward the eastern tip. A group of seals lay on the beach. A large male watched us warily. We kept our distance, but got close enough to see the females cuddled with their pups. Toward the back of the group, a mother with a red slash on her side caught my eye. "What do you think did that?"

"Shark, I bet," Roman said. "I've seen them circling around here. Even saw one grab a seal pup once."

I shuddered.

Mirra sucked in her breath. "Look!"

A young seal with the saddest eyes I'd ever seen had something wrapped around its neck and flippers. All the other seals hitched their clumsy bodies toward the water to escape. Roman stepped closer. "It looks like a gill net."

"Poor thing," Mirra said. "It's trapped."

Mirra and I moved closer too. I pulled out the knife. "Let's cut it free."

If we were starving, we would have killed it for food. And maybe I'd regret losing this food, but I pulled out the knife.

"I can do it," Roman said. I gave him the knife. "Mirra, you hold it. Annie, you help as best you can, okay?"

We nodded. "Okay."

At our lunge, the trapped seal barked and tried to thrash its tail. Mirra grabbed it around its middle and tried to pick it up, but it squirmed free. She tried again. This time she held it tight to her chest. I used my good arm to pin its tail against Mirra's body so it couldn't whip as much.

As Roman cut through the netting, Mirra said, "It looks starved."

We peeled away the tight strings, revealing raw wounds where the netting had cut into the seal's hide.

"There you go, little one," Mirra cooed, as the last of the net fell away. She set it down, and it immediately headed for the ocean, splashing into the water, diving beneath the waves.

"To be trapped like that." I winced.

After Roman returned the knife, he stared off at the water. That's when I realized I'd been wrong. The saddest eyes I'd ever seen didn't belong to the seal. They belonged to Roman.

* * *

We gathered driftwood and wound our way back to camp. Mirra and I talked, but Roman hardly said a word. What was he thinking about?

By the time we got the wood stacked, the sun was low in the sky. Roman sank onto the sand. He stretched out with his hands clasped behind his head like a cushion.

"Off to the latrine," I said. "I'll let you know about the smell of my pee."

"Ha!" Mirra called. "A joke! You actually made a joke."

I smirked at her, but I secretly relished the thought that I could be a light-hearted joke teller who made people laugh.

I decided to wash in the lake too. As I swished around, I let the quiet settle in and thought about all the changes I'd gone through.

When I neared camp, I saw that Roman had fallen asleep. I signaled to Mirra that I was going to check out his shelter. She nodded.

A short time later, I was studying the raft. Burn holes! They hadn't been here last time. I wasn't sure if it would have floated before, but I knew it wouldn't now. Roman had purposefully ruined a raft, a raft that might have helped us get to the mainland.

With new determination, I ducked inside his shelter. A life jacket. His ax. The calendar pole with forty or so notches. And a sizable piece of driftwood. I examined it. Oh my God! He'd used the knife to carve pictures.

Pictures that told a story.

Chapter Eighteen
Guts

The seagulls shrieked a warning cry. Roman might be outside!

I quickly set the carved driftwood back in the same spot where I'd found it and peeked out of his shelter. No sign of him.

Using a branch, I tried to erase my tracks leading to and away from his shelter. The fierce wind would help too.

When I arrived back at camp, I discovered Roman was still sleeping.

"Find anything?" Mirra asked.

"He's carved pictures in a piece of driftwood," I whispered. "One is of a girl with long hair, probably Tamara. Another of a mean looking man, and a tight fist."

Mirra touched her throat. "He could be hiding out here from the man."

Roman stirred and then sat up. He rubbed his eyes. "Sorry. I must have fallen asleep." He stood. "I'm shot. Sleep well, you two. See you in the morning." He stumbled off in the fading light.

"What if the man finds this place?" Mirra said. "Would he hurt us too?"

"Let's keep carrying a weapon," I said. "I'm not ruling out Roman as a danger, either." A cold breeze sent us shivering into our tent.

By the next morning, the temperature had dropped dramatically. Mirra and I both wore our jackets, but we were both chilled. Roman strode toward us, carrying a spear.

"I thought I'd try my luck spearing," he said. "I wouldn't mind standing around a warm fire and roasting some fresh fish. You two want to come?"

"Sure," I said. Mirra and I each grabbed a spear.

I was clumsy spearing with my left arm, but Roman and Mirra each got a fish.

On our way back to the fire, a fuzzy little tern chick scooted toward me.

"So cute!" Mirra said.

We spotted several more fluff-balls. They'd venture out, then dart back toward their scolding parent.

Suddenly, Roman said, "Look!" He pointed toward a black blob on the beach. "Something's dead."

We hurried toward it and soon saw that it was an adult seal. "Do you think it's safe to eat?" I asked.

Mirra sniffed the air. "It doesn't smell rotten."

"We could cut it up," I said, "and we'd have enough food for days. I wonder what killed it."

"A fight, I'm guessing," Mirra said.

Roman had turned green.

"Are you okay?" I asked.

"Uh, yeah."

My mind switched tracks. "We could try drying seal strips so we have food for the winter."

"Winter?" Mirra squeaked. "This cold snap is just a fluke. Winter is still far away, right?"

"It could be closer than we think," I said.

Roman still looked shaken, but he managed a nod. "The weather on islands can be unpredictable."

"Winter," Mirra repeated, hugging herself. The word hung icily in the air.

After a lengthy pause, Roman glanced toward the dead seal. "We'll need to build a drying rack and do the butchering. With Annie's hand, she should probably do the rack."

"And because you're squeamish," Mirra said, "that leaves me to butcher."

"I was hoping you'd volunteer." Roman waggled his eyebrows in a playful gesture, but it felt forced.

"I'm hungry enough to do it," Mirra said.

I handed her the knife and Roman passed me his ax.

Roman positioned the seal belly up. Its milky dead eyes caught the light. I caught Roman's expression. He had shrunk back and was pressing his tight fist against his chest and rubbing it as if to erase something. Over and over again.

Mirra hadn't noticed. Lips pressed together, she started at the throat and sliced down. I had to give her credit. Not even a squeal of disgust. Using both hands, Roman peeled the hide back. Mirra bent over to cut some more.

I walked off to gather poles, sticks, and something like rope for making the rack. Best to set it up by camp so we could watch that the birds or critters didn't steal the meat.

My sore wrist made jabbing posts in the sand a struggle, and it took a while to build the frame of four sets of X-posts. Finding the two cross poles took time too. Now, though, I just needed to find a piece of net and fit it to the frame. I decided to check the debris pile closest to Mirra and Roman so I could check in. I had found a chunk of netting close to them when I heard a stifled squeal. Or was it a scream?

I jogged toward them. I'd worked myself into a hysterical panic by the time I reached them.

"Hey, Annie." Mirra's hands and arms were covered with slime and blood, but she had a grin on her face making me sigh with relief. "This is disgusting," she shrieked. "We had to break open the ribs and scoop out the guts. I nearly lost it. The smell! Worse than the girls' locker room."

I smiled and kind of wished I could be helping.

They'd brought over a piece of canvas and had cleverly dragged the seal onto it to keep the meat from getting sandy.

"We've been talking," Roman said. "How about soaking most of the meat in a saltwater brine before roasting or drying it?"

I nodded. "I can take some pieces with me now and get them roasting."

"Sounds good," Roman said. "We're almost done here."

"I'll wait until later to clean up," Mirra said. She looked down at her shirt, stained with blood and gunk. "The producers of those romantic island movies ought to see us. Not much glamour here."

"If we make it back home and Hailey's mom and I make a YouTube video, I'm going to suggest we do some survival ones. I'll tell her you should star in *How to Gut a Seal.*"

"Ha! My claim to fame."

I left the two of them. I managed to carry chunks of meat and the heart and liver back to camp. Pulling and fastening the net on top of the rack was a major pain. If only I had the use of both hands. Finally I placed the meat on top for roasting. Mirra and Roman still weren't back.

When I finally caught sight of Roman, he was carrying a canvas-wrapped bloody mess. I drew in a startled breath. Mirra?

But no. Mirra, carrying the hide, came into view. I rubbed my forehead. Jumping to conclusions and letting my imagination go wild wasn't helping anything.

Roman placed the bloody seal meat in the cooler.

"Roman said if we get a bunch of hides, we could use one to make moccasins, boots, or clothes." Mirra was nearly giddy.

I remembered that Mirra had given up her shirt to pad my splint and now wore her mom's shirt. It was looking as worn as my T-shirt.

"When we get rescued," Mirra said, "we should start our own boutique line. *Annie and Mirra's Unique Castaway Island Creations.*"

I joined in the fun. "*Clothes durable enough for survival.*" I cocked my head. "Could our boutique also carry seal-hide blankets?"

"Most definitely." Mirra giggled.

Several gulls flew over, hoping to snatch a piece of seal meat.

"Get away," Mirra shrieked, waving her arms like a crazy scarecrow.

I knew the gulls stealing our food could devastate us, but when a bubble of laughter sprang up, I gave in to it. And, because it felt so good, I kept laughing. I waved my arms like a crazy scarecrow too.

"You two are lunatics," Roman called out, his voice light. "Hey, the drying rack turned out well."

"It's rickety, but it should do the job." I pointed to the tin on top of the fire. "The seal strips are nearly cooked."

"I'll just pound the supports in a little deeper. That had to be hard with your wrist."

While Roman did that, Mirra set the knife on a stump. "Off to wash."

"Okay." I examined the hide wondering how we might use it.

Roman finished pounding. "There," he said. "That should stay upright." He felt the knife blade. "We worry about the coming winter, but if this knife becomes useless, we're sunk."

I thought a moment about how much we depended on it. I stole a sideways glance at him. If he tried to stop us from signaling a rescue boat, would I have enough courage to use this knife on him? I hoped I wouldn't have to find out.

The sound of splashing turned my focus to the ocean. Mirra had waded in up to her neck in the ocean and was swishing her body when my tired brain kicked back into gear. Sharks! With her bloody arms, she could draw them right to her! I ran to shore, calling. "Mirra, get out of there."

"Annie!" She waded back to shore. "What's wrong?"

"Sharks can smell the blood."

"I was only up to my knees."

Feeling foolish, I let out a long breath. I really needed to get a grip.

"I'm tired," Mirra said, "but I feel kind of good too."

"You should," I said.

We each filled a cup with seal strips. Roman took the first bite. "Not bad. Could use hot sauce, though."

Mirra took a bite. "I'm thinking shrimp sauce."

I took a big bite. The seal meat was soft and rubbery, and tasted like the sea. Not terrible. "Barbecue sauce," I said, "with a side of French fries."

"Oh, yes," Mirra said. "French fries."

"My dad makes the best grilled shrimp," Roman said. "We sit around the grill and as soon as he says they're done, it's like a feeding frenzy."

If Mirra had been out deeper and a school of sharks had been near while she washed her bloody arms, we could have seen another feeding frenzy.

"And now for dessert," Roman said, after we'd eaten several strips. "The heart and liver roasted to perfection." He carefully cut them in thirds, serving Mirra first.

"Mmm, not bad," she said. "Rich tasting, like the duck."

"It's good," I agreed, "but I'm so tired I can hardly chew."

"I'm tired too," Roman said, rinsing out his cup. "See you in the morning." Roman was never one for long goodbyes.

Before going inside the tent, I opened the cooler, pulled out three small pieces of meat, and laid them on the rack.

"What are you doing?" Mirra asked.

"I want to see if they'll be safe from the gulls overnight. It'll be a major pain if we have to guard the meat until it dries."

"Smart idea," Mirra said.

She and I lay in the tent for several minutes before she spoke. "Do you think everyone's given up on the search?"

I guessed they had, but I said, "I doubt it."

"I wonder how Mom and Dad are doing." Mirra's voice cracked.

She had mentioned them not getting along, but we hadn't talked about it. "They're frantic."

"I actually meant their marriage."

I sat up. "I remember you telling me that your dad's sister drowned in a pond when she was little and your grandparents' marriage broke up soon after."

"Uh huh." Mirra sat up too. "Dad said things were never the same after that, especially when it came to his mom. My being lost could put them over the edge."

"How bad have things gotten?"

"Well, I haven't told you what I saw." It was half a minute before she continued. "I saw my mom, with another man, in the club's bar."

"What are you saying?"

"I don't know exactly other than they were eye to eye, intent on each other."

"Oh, Mirra. Do you know the guy?"

"I've seen him around the gym. I'm not sure how far they've taken this, and I doubt Dad has a clue. He's stuck in his own world most of the time."

"You didn't ask your mom about it?"

"No. I wanted to wait. I can tell you she watches her phone a lot and after getting texts, she often leaves to answer them. She also doesn't set her phone down where Dad might see her messages. If I'm being realistic, their marriage is probably over."

"Oh, Mirra, I'm sorry." I covered her hand with my own.

She clasped it and squeezed. "Hey, if she wants a divorce, it'll crush Dad and me. But you know what? We'll survive."

"Yes," I said. "You will."

As tired as I was, my mind wouldn't shut down. I hoped that Mirra's parents would work through things. But hope, like our drifting raft, fades away.

I awoke when I heard birds calling. Mirra was already out of the tent. I stumbled out of bed. This was day eleven.

The seal strips were gone. Three suspicious looking gulls flew overhead.

Mirra returned with firewood. "The birds are probably getting back at us for taking their eggs."

Roman strode into view. With his mussed hair, he looked sinister. He waved a handful of leaves. "Does everyone want tea?"

I could have laughed aloud, but managed to contain it. "Tea would be lovely," I said with a British accent.

While he worked on tea, I explained how I'd tested out a couple of strips overnight. "I don't think they stole it during the night, but in the early morning."

"So we'll be okay if someone gets up early," Roman said.

"I wonder if we could make a scarecrow," I said.

"That's a good idea." Roman nodded.

"Or we could move the rack over the fire," Mirra said, "speed things along, and have them dried by nighttime."

"That's a great idea!" Roman slapped her a high-five.

I nodded, wishing I'd thought of it.

We spent the morning cutting strips, placing them on the rack, flipping them over after an hour or so of heat, and guarding them from the gulls. Midday, Roman said, "Let's take a break. Do you want more tea for lunch?"

Mirra and I both nodded. But I had to secretly shake my head. How was it that the man who continued to lie to us and threaten our possible rescue was also such a huge help and was now making us tea?

Roman built up the fire and added leaves to the pot. "This needs to steep."

Steep? I never knew how to feel around Roman. He could be scary at times but right now I wanted to laugh. How many evil villains talk about steeping tea?

Roman might have noticed my head-shake because he shrugged. "My mom's a tea drinker." He turned to Mirra. "It's getting warm. If Annie will guard the meat, maybe we should have another swim lesson?"

"Okay," Mirra said. "Thanks."

Roman poured three cups of tea in our plastic cups. When he handed me mine, I took a whiff. Mmm, strawberry.

We each grabbed several dried seal strips. After a few moments of silence, Mirra said, "So, Roman, we know your mom likes tea, but what's she like?"

Roman's eyes clouded over. "She's ... intense." He walked over to pour me more tea.

As he filled my cup, I couldn't help staring at his hands. Bruises and dirty, broken nails showed how much he'd been helping. Still, I couldn't let myself forget that these same hands could have waved to our families, sending us on the rescue boat home.

"If it's all right," I said, after finishing eating, "I'd like to take a bath before you two do your swim lesson."

"Go ahead," Mirra said. "I'll help Roman get another batch drying."

"When we get back home," I called, "maybe along with the boutique you could open *Unique Castaway Island Cuisine.*"

Mirra nodded. "I'm liking it. We'll feature sensational seal strips."

On the way to the pond, I imagined what our lives would be like if we got to return home. Once Mirra was back with Brittany and the others, would she be tempted to freeze me out again? Would I be more careful about making her feel stupid?

Goldilocks and Little Guy were grazing nearby. When I slowly walked toward them, Goldilocks lifted her head and looked ready to bolt. She remembered and was on high alert. I retreated wondering if my damage could ever be forgiven.

At the pond, I stripped off my T-shirt. I kept thinking about Mirra's and my relationship. We'd been through so much together. Girls who depended on one another to survive were sure to stay close.

I shed my shorts and underwear next. I realized I'd been due to get my period a week ago, but it hadn't come. Probably from the stress and lack of food. I doubted Mirra would get hers either.

I stepped into the calm water and looked at my reflection. My body had changed, becoming more defined and muscular, but it was my posture that made me most proud. Arms flung out wide and head thrown back, ready to tackle whatever lay ahead.

CHAPTER NINETEEN
PARTY TIME

D ays went by. With the dried seal strips, we could grab a quick meal if we wanted. I didn't want to think about whether we should be saving them for the winter. For once, I wanted to be carefree.

Roman and Mirra had daily swim lessons. On an especially warm and windy morning, they took off together. Here was my chance to snoop in Roman's shelter and see if anything had changed.

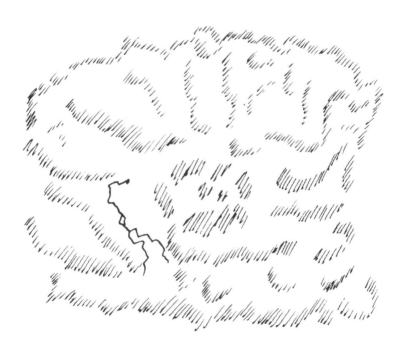

I jogged until I caught sight of his tepee. Trying to make as few footprints as possible, I ducked between the gap in poles. Everything looked the same, except the story stick. He had added one more picture. After the fist, he'd carved a man lying face up, eyes closed. What was that supposed to mean? A crack of thunder told me I better hurry back to camp.

Once there, I had hoped to find Mirra alone, but Roman strode toward me. "What have you been doing?" he asked.

"I was, uh, checking on the seals." Could he see me blushing?

"Oh, so you saw?" Roman's heavy eyebrows rose.

"Saw what?" My heart raced. Did he know I'd been snooping?

"The lightning." He kept studying me.

"Oh, no I missed it."

"We had to cut our lesson short. Lightning struck the inside of a cloud and lit it up."

Mirra poked her head out from the tent. "Yes," Mirra called, "it would have been even cooler if it was darker out."

"There!" Roman pointed. "It happened again."

"Wow." My breath caught. "Kind of like our own fireworks show."

We kept watching. "The cloud looks like the inside of clam shells when the sun hits them," Mirra said.

I caught movement out of the corner of my eye. Goldilocks and her yearling, Little Guy, ambled toward us. She probably wouldn't let me get close again, but she seemed to have forgiven me. Little Guy's mane was tousled, reminding me of Joey's hair when he first got up. "Hey," I said suddenly, "anyone know the date?"

"June twenty-third," Roman answered, adding more driftwood to the fire.

"It's my brother Joey's birthday."

"How old is he?" Roman asked.

"Nine." I swallowed. "Just before I left, he asked me to talk to Dad about his getting a puppy. He'd been on the Humane society website and had one picked out." My chin trembled. "I wonder if he got it."

Splashing drew my eye. Little Guy, head lowered to the ocean, pawed the water with one hoof, making me laugh.

As Little Guy played, I wondered again about the horses. How had they gotten here? Did anyone know about them? Was Sea Stallion leading me to water and saving our lives a fluke or was it something more?

Mirra interrupted my thoughts. "Remember when we were eight or nine and played Statue Makers where you spin people around and they pretend to be someone?"

"Joey always pretended to be a puppy," I finished for her.

"One time we played, and Ryan was at your house. He pretended to be a deep-sea fisherman pulling in a trophy fish."

"Good memory! Ryan's always been obsessed with fishing."

Mirra stole a sideways look at me. She moved closer so Roman couldn't hear. "He wasn't interested in me, was he?"

I shrugged. I wasn't going to hurt her and say he was probably more interested in Brittany. "Actually," I said, "the boat's motor had most of his attention."

"Ha! Just my luck."

I wondered how our disappearance had affected Ryan. Had my aunt and uncle wanted him to come back home? Or was he helping Dad and my brothers deal with all this?

"Let's celebrate Joey's birthday with a party." Mirra called to where Roman stirred the fire. "How about it, Roman?"

"I'm always up for a party," Roman said. "I'll steep tea." He waggled his eyebrows again.

Mirra laughed. "Oooo, when we're back on the mainland, we are so going to tell your buddies. You'll never live down this tea-steeping thing."

I noticed the woodpile was low and set off to find a few pieces of dry wood. As I carried them back in my jacket, I wondered if Dad and the boys were celebrating Joey's birthday. I had promised Joey I'd bake his favorite cake, Black Forest. I hope Dad thought to buy one.

Mirra hiked back from the north beach, one hand behind her back. Before I could ask her what she was hiding, she darted behind the tent. After Roman added the leaves to our warm water and I added wood to our fire, Mirra reappeared. "Shall we start the party with our, uh, seal nachos?"

A flock of curious tern chicks testing their wings joined our party. Mirra, Roman, and I watched one struggle to stay in the air. It kept falling. *Flap, flap, thunk. Flap, flap, thunk.* The fifth time, it flew along with the others.

Tern eggs, I mused. Our first food. Without the eggs, we wouldn't have lasted this long.

Roman brought in a third sitting log and arranged them so they made a triangle. As thick clouds moved in and the dunes changed from their golden hue to shadowy purples, we filled our green cups and gathered in front of the fire.

I took a bite of the dried seal strip. This piece tasted like gamey liver stew and had a fishy aftertaste, but it filled my belly, and washing it down with strawberry tea helped.

Mirra sat back, looking at the sky. I followed her lead.

Several minutes later, Mirra whispered, "So I have another topic, and I know we're partying, but this topic's serious."

"O-kay," I said.

"Since becoming shipwrecked, I've thought a lot about, well, dying, and you probably have too," she said. "So the topic is heaven. If you believe in one, what is it like?" She turned her head toward me and asked shyly, "Do you want to go first, Annie?"

"I guess." Breathe in, breathe out. "I like to imagine a heaven where I can see Mom again. I know I'm supposed to want to see God, but to tell you the truth..." I swallowed. "I want to see my mom more."

Mirra nodded. "It has to be so hard." We stayed quiet for a long while. "I kind of miss going to church," Mirra continued. "We stopped going after Grandma moved away."

"My family goes to church every week," Roman said, "but it's more for show."

"Who are they trying to impress?" Mirra asked.

Roman took a bite of seal. "The community. My dad is a judge."

I nodded. "And do you believe in heaven?" I prompted.

He took a long time to answer. "Let's just say I believe in hell."

Mirra and I exchanged glances.

Roman quickly changed the subject. "Mirra, you didn't answer the heaven question."

Mirra rubbed her chin. "I hadn't thought much about God before now, but I'm with Annie. I hope there's life after death. What I really hope is that we can make our own heaven. It would be filled with all the things we love." She stood. "That reminds me. I made you something, Annie." She ducked into the tent and returned with a clam shell necklace.

I stood up. A flood of emotion washed over me, and I had to bend over pretending to examine the three pinkish shells she'd strung with heavy net string so she wouldn't see my face. The shells caught the sunlight and shimmered. When I could speak, I said, "It's beautiful. You do have a knack for making things like this. Thank you." I widened my arms and shyly looked at her. She hurried toward me and flung her arms around me. We held each other a long time.

When we finally drew apart, I slipped the necklace over my head, fluffing out my hair and not talking to anyone in particular, asked, "How do I look?"

"Beautiful," Roman said. "You should wear clam shells more often. They bring out the highlights in your hair." He winked. "Off to try for fish. I'm getting mighty tired of seal strips."

I swept my hair out of my eyes so I could watch as he walked away. Thinking about his comment about how I looked beautiful made my cheeks flush. I turned away but not soon enough.

"Annie, are you falling for Roman?"

"No."

"I don't believe you."

"Well, I mean he's a good-looking guy, but he could be trouble with a capital T. It's just that ... "

"What?"

Did I dare share this? "I ... I've never had a boy tell me I'm beautiful." I squirmed. "I've never felt very beautiful."

"You are beautiful, Annie." She motioned to the stump. "Sit down and let me French-braid your hair."

I sat. Mirra began by massaging my scalp. I immediately relaxed and transported myself to another day. I was a bit older, wore an emerald green dress, and had styled my hair with the clip. My date didn't look anything like Nick, whom I hadn't thought about for days.

This young man had dark features and the voice of a country western singer. He and I had spent the evening at a fancy party and now it was time to say goodnight. My date leans toward me and says that I have the most incredible sea-green eyes. He likes the way I'd fixed my hair but wondered if he could unclip it. After my nod, he lets my hair flow down. He looks deep into my eyes and says, "Oh Annie, you are so beautiful." He leans in close and—

"You seem miles away," Mirra said.

I laughed. "Yes, I'm relaxed."

Mirra's skilled hands began the braiding next. My mind flitted to ways people show love. I show Joey love by reading to him. He shows me love by snuggling in. Steven takes the bread crusts because he knows I don't like them. Dad makes sure I'm safe and worries about me. These were all wonderful, but so was the "I think you're beautiful" boyfriend kind of love and the "Let me French-braid your hair" kind of love.

"My masterpiece is complete," Mirra said in a teasing voice. "You look fab-u-lous, mar-ve-lous, divine actually."

"Ha!" But I patted it and could tell how pretty it must look. "If I had two hands, I'd try to do yours."

"No worries. I think we're in for a thunderstorm. I might stand out in it and give my hair the rainwater treatment."

I studied the building surf and the purplish sky.

"Oh, to have shampoo." Mirra moaned.

"Do you know anything about making soap?"

"Not really."

"I think it involves using animal fat and lye that survivalists get from soaking ashes. It takes a long time too."

"If we ever figure it out, we'll have to add Castaway Island Soap to our boutique line."

"You know," I said, my tone more serious, "I could see you having your own salon or boutique someday. Maybe you'll design jewelry and sell it in your store."

"Thanks for saying that." Mirra suddenly smiled. "Speaking of shampoo, do you remember when we were little and Grandma put us in the bathtub and washed our hair?"

"I do. She'd shape it into hairstyles and name it things like the Miss America Swirl, the Mohawk, or the Punk Rocker's Spikes. We'd laugh so hard!" After a pause, I said, "I miss your grandma."

Mirra nodded. "Grandma..." Her voice trailed off. "This has to be killing her too." She stared past the grasses and dunes to the ocean. "It's been almost three weeks. I wonder if they're thinking about having a funeral for us."

I stood next to her and together we faced the oncoming waves.

* * *

F acing the waves. We were still standing close together when Mirra touched her arm. "Annie." Her voice quavered. "Look at this." She pointed to a dark, purplish spot on her forearm.

"What is it?"

"It's the spot my dermatologist said I should keep my eye on. It's gotten bigger and the color has changed. And it's scaly."

Skin cancer? I couldn't form the words. And it was growing?

"This is exactly what he said to watch for," Mirra said. "I was supposed to call him immediately. He named a fast-growing skin cancer."

"Oh, Mirra." My mind couldn't register at first. All I could do was put my arm around her.

Cancer.

Fast growing.

This couldn't be happening.

Mirra pulled away, fear in her eyes. "I'm going to get out of the sun. Maybe take a nap. I feel tired all of a sudden."

"Okay. You go rest." I watched her go. I'd seen this before. Mirra shut down the same way when a favorite uncle had died. It was how she dealt with things. I could only think to pray. I clasped my hands. *Please, oh, please, God. Help her. She needs to get to a doctor. Help us get home.*

I paced around the camp. Skin cancer! I didn't know much about it other than it had to be taken care of quick. I ran my hands through my hair. If not treated, did it keep spreading until it hit an organ like the brain or heart? I felt chilled from head to toe. We needed to get off this island quickly!

Was there any way we could patch the raft Roman had burned? Maybe find pitch and fill the holes with—I don't know—seaweed? But we didn't know anything about the current and couldn't paddle it well. No, taking off in the raft would be suicide. Still ...

A thunderhead loomed in the distance. Roman arrived as a chilly rain sliced down. He had speared two fish, which we quickly added to the cooler. "Roman, come inside the tent. We need to talk."

"You look so serious," he said, once we were inside.

The rain kept pinging on the tent roof, Mirra showed him her arm. "I'm worried it's skin cancer and it will keep growing."

He narrowed his eyes. "Someone your age getting skin cancer?" Using his thumb, he rubbed at the mark.

I glared at him. Had he wanted to see if we'd used berry juice to make the mark in order to get his sympathy? What was with this guy? I wanted answers from him. Now!

Mirra, to her credit, didn't snarl back. "It's in my family history. An uncle got it when he was young too, but he caught it in time. I'll be sure to wear long sleeves. Now let's talk about something else."

I felt this urgency to do something or to at least find out answers. "Would it help take your mind off of things if we played *Deep Secret*?" I asked.

"Yeah, let's play. You pick the topic, Annie."

I zeroed in. "Something we regret doing. It should be a major regret."

Mirra shifted uncomfortably and opened her mouth, but it took a moment for her to speak. "I'm not going to talk about what I did to Annie because this isn't the time. Instead, I want to tell about getting a D for the fourth quarter in math."

The rain pelted out, and I had to lean toward Mirra to hear. She hesitated, then finally began. "Mr. Ricker told me if I failed the final, I'd fail the course. He gave me a practice final." She ran a finger over the spot on her forearm. "I, uh, I found out from Brittany, whose brother had been in the same trouble the year before, that the practice final had some of the same test questions on it. So I... so I used a calculator, wrote the answers on the inside of my arm, and went to class."

Mirra kept looking at her arm. "I got a C on the test, but I think Mr. Ricker knew I cheated. He asked me to explain how I'd gotten one of the right answers, and I mumbled something. He stared at me for the longest time. Finally, he said I could go. I remember he called after me to be careful. We'd just gotten freezing rain, so I told myself he was talking about the roads, but I knew he wasn't."

Mirra lifted her gaze. "That night I couldn't sleep. I couldn't tell him what I'd done, but I decided that I would never cheat again."

I thought back to the times I made her feel stupid. Did she see herself as being dumb? That must feel awful.

"You learned from it," I said. "That's what's important."

Mirra nodded. She turned toward Roman. "Do you want to go next?"

"Not really," he said, but he rubbed his forehead in thought. "Okay, I have one," he finally announced. "Our backyard has a lot of oak trees, and the squirrels are pretty tame. I was little, maybe seven, and I'd made friends with a gray squirrel, Scamper. I rigged up a live trap and he was so tame I caught him right away. I put him in a huge fish aquarium and made sure the cover was on tight. I gave him peanuts and water, but he kept scratching to get out."

Roman stared toward the tent's doorway. "One day I came home from school and he was lying on his side, dead." His shoulders slumped. "It's one of my biggest regrets." He rubbed his right knuckles, over and over.

"That would make a person feel bad," Mirra said.

She and I exchanged glances. We might still be figuring out how to forgive one another, but on this point, we were in sync. Roman must have bigger regrets than what he was telling.

"Your turn, Annie." Mirra's gentle tone reminded me of Mom's. The rain pattering on the canvas, gentler now, and the semi-darkness somehow made it easier to talk. "My biggest regret," I began, "was the way I left the house... the day my mom died." I pictured the snowy morning with my dad shoveling the sidewalk and my brothers getting ready for school. "Joey couldn't find his book bag and my mom asked me to help him. I barked something back about us babying him. Then I left for the bus. Not a *good-bye*," I continued in a choked whisper, "or a *see you later*. I just walked out the door."

Mirra reached over to squeeze my hand. "Your mom knew you loved her, Annie."

I nodded. The rain stopped and a ribbon of light peeked under the tent almost as if Mom was sending me a message.

Roman rose to a crouch position. "Rain's stopped. I'll cook those fish tomorrow." He threw open the tent flap. "Goodnight." But he didn't move right away. "I'm glad you talked me into playing. It helps to know everyone has feelings of guilt."

I wished I knew exactly what he meant.

Mirra and I followed him outside. While Mirra banked the fire, I watched the setting sun filter through the vanishing storm clouds. If heaven existed, and Mom was up in heaven, could she see me? Did she know I was stranded? Would I be able to see her again one day and tell her I'm sorry I didn't say goodbye?

I searched for Sea Stallion, but a cloud blocked out the sinking sun and turned the world into shadows.

Chapter Twenty
The Island Speaks

I woke to the sound of Mirra crawling out of the tent. "Wow," she said, "it's so foggy I can't even see our sitting logs."

It reminded me of the day our families—most likely my dad and Mirra's parents—had arrived and left before we could signal them. "I'm heading to the beach where I can watch for boats. But first, let's see your arm."

It looked as scaly and purplish-red as yesterday. "What did you think of Roman's reaction yesterday? Did you see how he touched it and then looked at his thumb to check if something had smeared off?"

"Yes, as if I would fake something like this." Mirra groaned. "I have to go to the latrine. I hope I can find it."

I walked through the heavy fog and searched the horizon for boats, but it was impossible to see. I didn't hear any unusual sounds, so I returned to camp.

An hour or so passed and Mirra still hadn't returned. I added wood to the embers and then cupped my hands. "Mirra?" I called.

No answer. I looked toward Roman's shelter, but it was like trying to see through frothy milk. He probably wouldn't come until he could see.

I called again with no answer. Dread hung over me. Was she lost? "Mirra!" My cry sliced through the heavy air.

I only heard the pounding surf, then a slight movement. A swishing sound. I jerked around. A sparrow scooted through the grass. Take a breath, I told myself.

Gulls squawked, sounding like warning cries. What could have happened to her? I kept calling and walking. Was I heading the wrong way? I felt disoriented, as if I'd been blindfolded and spun around ten times.

My foot stumbled over something hard. I whimpered, my imagination on overload. I peered down. It was only a chunk of driftwood. Enough with the crazy thoughts. I had to get a grip.

Maybe I should head back to camp. Could I even find it?

I'd never been in fog this dense. Even though it must be late morning, I couldn't see the sun. "Mirra," I called again.

"Annie!" Her voice was faint. "I'm over here."

My heart leaped. "Are you okay?"

"I ... I couldn't find my way back."

"Keep talking."

"I'm this way."

Seconds later, I grabbed Mirra in a fierce hug. "I called and called for you."

Mirra pulled away. "I didn't hear you. The surf and the gulls must have been too loud. I don't know where we are."

"I'm mixed up now too. Let's stay put for a while."

"Okay," Mirra said in a small voice.

We sat side by side. I could finally breathe normally again. "It was foggy like this the day of Mom's wake," I whispered. "Driving was awful."

"Still, tons of people came," Mirra said. "I spent most of the time talking to Hailey's mom."

"I like her. Have you ever seen their backyard with the little bridge over the water garden? She's so creative."

Mirra nodded. "You talked about her teaching a class."

"Yeah. She wanted me and Hailey to help with YouTube tutorials."

"At your mom's funeral, she asked me what I thought she could do for you."

"That sounds like her." I nodded. "She told me to call her anytime I needed to talk or wanted a break."

"That's really nice. I'm glad, especially," Mirra's voice cracked, "especially since I wasn't there for you then." Mirra stood. She opened her arms, and I stepped in. It might have been because of the cover of fog, or it might have been that we desperately needed this, but we clung together for a long time.

After we drew apart, I quickly wiped at my eyes. I think Mirra might have too.

"*E-he-eee-uhn-uhn-uhn.*"

"What's that?" Mirra turned to face the sound.

"The horses! I bet they're heading to the pond. Yes, I hear splashing. If the pond is that way, I know directions. Come on."

I led the way through the soupy mess; Mirra walked close by. To stay calm, I counted our steps. "Twenty-nine... thirty... thirty-one." On the fortieth step, I saw the glow from the fire. And the tent!

"Hoorah!" I cried.

The fog lifted slightly. We sat and munched on seal strips. By early afternoon, the fog had almost disappeared. Roman strode toward us. "You two okay?" he asked.

"Grab some food and have a seat," Mirra said. "We have a story to tell you."

By late afternoon, the fog had disappeared. A band of four horses walked past, including Little Guy. I didn't spot his mom, though.

I heard a seal barking and said, "Hey, want to check on the seals? Maybe we'll see the one we rescued."

"Sure," Mirra said.

"I'll bring the spear and net along," Roman said, rubbing his peeling nose.

Mirra suddenly said, "Give me the knife, Annie. I'm going to try to make a hat."

While Roman and I speared fish, Mirra cut a piece of canvas. The fishing was easy for once and we had three big ones by the time she'd formed the canvas into a three-cornered hat. "Try it, Roman," she said. "You'll look like a pirate."

I couldn't decide if it made him look scary or funny.

He rubbed his chin. "Pirates should be able to grow beards, and I just have this stubble."

"Maybe we could get you a friendly parrot," I said, "or at least a tern who would sit on your shoulder."

Mirra nodded. "Let's hear your pirate growl."

"*Aaaarrrrgggghhhh!*"

Mirra laughed, and I joined in.

"You were so good at that," Mirra said.

"My sister was Captain Hook and hounded me to practice with—" He suddenly froze.

"You have a sister?" Mirra asked.

He wiped his hands on his shorts. "Two, actually."

"You never mentioned them." Mirra kept her voice friendly.

"I don't like talking about them because, well, it's hard."

I could tell Mirra wanted to press, but she only asked their names.

"My little sister is Miranda and my twin is Tamara."

Tamara. So the picture in his wallet wasn't a girlfriend.

"Let's carry these back and I'll fix them." Roman started toward camp.

A cool breeze made me shiver, and my tone changed. "Hey guys," I said, "how about taking a side trip." I pointed toward the clam flats where a group of seals sunned themselves. "If we're still here in winter," my words hung in the air, "we might have to figure out a way to kill a seal."

Mirra cringed. "Is there a chance we could survive a winter on this island?"

"There's always a chance," I said. "Especially, if we have each other."

We were walking across a dune, halfway to the seals, when a glint of metal in the sand caught my eye. I picked it up. "Look at this."

We all bent over to study the small piece of tarnished metal. "It reminds me of a boy's shoe buckle I saw at a museum," Roman said.

I flipped it over. "It's old, all right."

"Maybe there's more," Mirra said.

We got on our knees. Roman and Mirra, with two good hands, scooped more sand than me, but I spotted a second treasure. "A coin!"

I handed it to Mirra, who brushed it off.

"Maybe it's a pirate treasure," Mirra said.

"Here's another one!" Roman said. He wiped it off. The date's hard to read—1760 maybe—and there's a king on one side and a queen on the other."

"Let's keep digging. Oh!" I held out two heavy, round balls.

"Musket balls, I bet." Roman dug deeper. "Another coin!"

Sand flew. Was that all? Then something white. A bone! The size of a human finger. I swallowed a scream.

"Part of a skeleton?" Roman asked, shrinking back.

I nodded, trying to breathe.

"I wonder who he ... or she ... was." Mirra said. She leaned closer to examine the bone.

"And how he or she died," I said. "Maybe the rest of him—or her—is under here. I bit my bottom lip.

"Do you suppose ... if we keep digging, we'd find a map or letters or a diary?" Mirra asked.

"Maybe," I said. "Do you ... do you want to keep digging?"

Roman and Mirra nodded.

We knelt by the bone and dug deeper. Strangely, as we uncovered a human hand, the wind died down, the waves quieted, and the birds stopped singing. We brushed sand away from the long bone of the upper arm next, then the shoulder, and lastly the skull. My own scalp prickled. I stared at the eye sockets, nose hole, and teeth.

"It's small." Roman's voice cracked. "This was a kid." He kept digging. "Look!" He picked up a button and brushed it off. "I bet this came from a boy's coat.

Maybe he was a cabin boy on a ship, or a young soldier."

"I wonder if his family ever found out what happened to him." Mirra wrapped her arms around herself. "He could have been our age and here all alone. Maybe he was shipwrecked too." Mirra studied Roman. "What do you think?"

Roman's Adam's apple bobbed as he swallowed. It took him a while to answer, but when he did, his voice was steady. "Hard to say. He could have died of starvation or the cold."

Like we might, I thought, gritting my teeth for the hundredth time as I thought of how Roman could have signaled our families that foggy day. He'd put his fears, whatever they were, ahead of our lives.

Mirra kept staring at the bones. "I'll make a marker for him."

I shivered, wondering if there were more hidden skeletons in the sand.

Roman was still examining the coins, musket balls, buckle, and button.

"Let's bring these back to camp," Mirra said.

I nodded. "They could come in handy for starting a fire, if we ever find flint."

Mirra reached for them and Roman handed over the artifacts. "I'd like to research them once we're back home," she said.

Roman didn't answer but gently reburied the bones.

"I'll get a board from the debris pile so we can make a marker," I said. As I walked, I thought about the next person coming to this island, finding the marker, and possibly discovering our dead bodies. I shivered.

Back at camp, Mirra used the knife and a charcoal stick to make the letters R.I.P.

Mirra and Roman dug the board deep in the sand. "Rest in Peace," I whispered.

I glanced up toward the heavens. *Are you resting in peace, Mom? Of course you're not, with everything so messed up.*

The three of us were quiet as we hiked toward the seals again and reached a high spot with a view.

"Look at that big one," Roman said a few minutes later. "It's swimming so far from—"

"Shark!" I pointed at a fin closing in on the seal. I held my breath as a group of seagulls flew off, circling. They knew what was about to happen! The seal leaped out of the water. The jaws of the shark opened. But just as the shark snapped, the seal did a back flip.

Ha! I let out a quick breath. It escaped!

"Go, seal!" Mirra cried. Only it wasn't over yet. The shark's fin zeroed in. The seal jumped through the air again, but this time the shark hit its target. Blood sprayed. Only the seal's thrashing head was visible sticking out of the shark's mouth.

I closed my eyes, but I could hear the seagulls circling in to snatch some meat. Circling, like the awful things that kept happening to us.

Mirra moaned.

I moved closer, wrapping an arm around her waist. Roman wrapped his arm around her on the other side. We stood there in silence until the last bird had finished snatching up bits of the seal from the water.

The wind picked up and, as we hiked back to camp, the sand beneath me seemed to shift. The hair at the back of my neck rose. How many tragedies had this island seen? Life vs. death. Death vs. life.

More sand swirled around my feet and settled. We were okay for now, I told myself.

For now, the sand seemed to taunt. *For now*.

Chapter Twenty-One
Life, Liberty, and the Pursuit of Truth

Days passed, shifting about like restless sand-bars, and June became July. The spot on Mirra's arm changed shape again and got even bigger. Mirra was quieter than usual, and I could only imagine the thoughts and worries that must be tumbling around in her head.

I remembered hearing about a woman doctor stranded in Antarctica who developed breast cancer. She had to perform a biopsy surgery on herself. I shook my head. No way could any of us dare do something like that for Mirra. We had to get to the mainland.

I glanced toward the grasses where several horses grazed. I couldn't help thinking that our salvation was somehow tied to the horses.

Toward the end of July, the spot on Mirra's arm had tripled in size. Although it was often on my mind, and I'm sure Mirra's too, we rarely talked about it. I couldn't tell what Roman thought of it. I wasn't about to argue with him over it, though. I'd learned from Mirra's and my fight that if we wanted to survive, we needed to band together, just like the horses do on a cold, wintry day.

We got another cold spell that lasted for three days. I pictured the horses needing to paw through the snow this winter to look for grass. Would they find enough to prevent starvation? Did we need to start making warm clothing?

As Mirra and I stockpiled wood, foraged for food, and kept the fire burning, the threats of winter and Mirra's skin cancer hung over us like fog. Mirra and I had set up more signal fires on the eastern and western ends and on the north and south beach. But we could do no more.

Roman didn't give Mirra or me any more hints as to his past or his motive for ignoring the rescue boat, and although I'd made one more secret search of his tent, I didn't find anything that answered my questions.

August 3rd was an especially chilly day, and we spent it stockpiling driftwood. That afternoon, Roman pulled a bunch of tall grass and said, "I'm going to try to insulate my shelter."

When he returned about an hour later, we talked about making a needle out of bone and figuring out thread so we could make leggings or boots. We also brainstormed how to make candles, soap, or a lantern.

Roman greeted us the next morning by saying, "Happy Fourth of August." I paused in my fire tending.

"We totally missed celebrating the Fourth of July," Mirra said. "How about celebrating it today? We could have a picnic and pretend to watch fireworks."

Steven had always loved fireworks. A month or so after Mom had died, he'd snuck out of the house. When Dad discovered him missing, he cased the neighborhood. He'd found Steven shooting off illegal fireworks with an older kid.

Did Dad have the energy to keep track of Steven this summer, or was my disappearance sapping all of his time? Had he missed a lot of work? Had they done anything fun? And with school starting in a month, would he have time to help the boys shop for back to school supplies and clothes?

"Annie?" Mirra asked.

"Uh, yeah. Independence Day. We should celebrate."

Mirra laughed. "When you think about it, we're as independent as it gets. We're free to decide how late we want to stay out or how much we want to work. And we don't have any rules."

We were free all right. Free to be lazy and starve to death, or to work hard and try to survive.

Roman picked up a spear. "I'll see if I can get a fish for our feast." He strode off.

I stared out at the rolling surf. "I wonder if my family went to Aunt Judy's Fourth of July picnic." My voice cracked. "They got a pontoon in April and talked about inviting us to watch the fireworks."

Mirra looked toward the ocean too. "The night before we shipwrecked, Brittany talked about bringing fireworks to Picnic Island. She was going to ask Natalie's brother to pick some up."

I could picture Brittany and Mirra talking that night. They probably also debated about whether they had to include me.

Mirra hung her head. "I'd been wrong, Annie, to put boys and Brittany ahead of you."

I nodded. "That's all in the past, Mirra. It's time to look toward the future."

"I sure hope Brittany or the others never went out that day," she said, gently running a thumb over her cancerous spot. "Brittany's dad was going to drive them, so hopefully he had enough sense. More sense than me," she whispered.

With the fire blazing, Mirra poured water in the tin and set it on to heat. Next, she pulled strawberry leaves from the cooler.

"You know," I said, "you're a huge help around here. I wish your mom and dad could see you."

Mirra licked her lips. It took her a while before she spoke. "I heard Mom and Dad talking last New Year's. They thought I was still listening to music, but I'd come into the kitchen for a snack and overheard them. Dad said that I didn't have a clue about how the real world works, that they'd babied me." Mirra's voice choked. "My mom usually stands up for me, but this time she didn't say anything. Dad told her how he'd tried to show me how to check pressure on a car tire, but I hadn't paid attention. Which was true. If we survive this, I'm going to pay attention to practical things."

"Hey," I said, "wait until they hear you caught a duck and butchered a seal."

Mirra smiled back. "Those were useful things, for sure. I might even put them on my job application."

I laughed.

"If we get back home," Mirra said, "next summer I want to apply for jobs. Maybe I'll try for clothing stores or a boutique. Get some experience before I open up my own."

"That sounds like a great plan."

Roman returned empty-handed. "Sorry, ladies. I didn't get a single fish. I think we should settle for dried seal and take a hike."

There were only seven strips of seal left. I passed out one to each of us. "That's almost the end," I said.

We ate in silence.

Roman stood up and grabbed the tin. "Let's take the north-shore route," he said. "Something different."

Mirra and I stood up. Mirra rubbed her legs before we set off.

"Are your legs sore?" I asked.

"A little. It's probably from yesterday's hike." Mirra turned to Roman. "My mom would be proud. She'd been nagging me about getting more exercise." Mirra laughed. "Mom got her wish." Mirra blew her long bangs out of her face. "My mom's a fitness instructor. She met my dad on a cruise ship." Mirra got a faraway expression on her face. She blinked, finally, then turned to Roman. "So, how about your parents? Your father's a judge?"

Roman stared at the ground, even though we were walking on sand and there wasn't anything to trip over. "Yeah, elected when I was seven." He lifted his head. The muscles in his jaw twitched.

"And what about your mom?" Mirra's voice was encouraging.

"Stay-at-home mom who didn't really want kids."

Mirra and I exchanged glances and then Mirra asked, "So you were planning on going away to college I'm guessing?"

"Yale, or that's what my mother wanted. I told her I wanted to be a landscape architect. You can guess how well that went over." He snorted. "Last summer, I worked for a landscaper, Gary. Great guy. I told my parents how much I liked the work and how I wanted to go back this summer, but my mother wouldn't have it. She threatened to shut down Gary's business. And since he hired illegal immigrants, she probably could have." He choke-laughed and his voice turned fake-cheery. "Of course, that isn't much of an issue any more."

"Yale," Mirra murmured, hurrying to catch up to us. "So do they want you to be a lawyer or something?"

"Anything that's prestigious. Definitely not digging in the dirt and spreading manure."

I wanted him to keep talking, but an awful smell made me pause. "Speaking of manure," I said, "do you smell that? Rotten fish or something else that's dead."

"What's that lump behind those bushes?" Mirra led the way. "Oh, no!"

Heart hammering, I looked past her to a bloated horse lying motionless on its side. Flies buzzed around the body. The long, blonde mane rippled in the wind. "It's Goldilocks," I said, swallowing.

"Do you think she died of old age?" Mirra asked.

"She had longer hair," I said, "like old horses seem to have."

"I wonder what happened to her yearling." Mirra searched the dunes.

Roman waved flies away from his face. "Let's get out of here."

Mirra and Roman backed away, but I stared. "We could think about getting the hide." I grimaced at the thought. "Use it for a blanket."

"Let's not," Roman said, looking like he could gag. "It smells like it's been here a while. It's not worth it."

If he planned on having to survive here this winter, he'd think it'd be worth it. But I couldn't muster up the heart for hacking away at Goldilocks. A thought flashed in my head. The horse was big enough that a helicopter could probably see it. Like they could see a *HELP* message if we wrote it big enough. I tapped my head with my fist. "I can't believe we haven't thought of this."

"What?" Mirra asked.

"We need to write *HELP* in the sand so a helicopter or plane flying overhead will spot it."

"But the wind will blow it smooth in minutes," Mirra said.

"No," I said, "we'll use things like heavy driftwood or poles."

"Hey, yeah," Mirra said.

"It should be someplace high." I turned toward Roman, wondering if he'd volunteer to help.

"I'll go back to camp and check the fire," he said. "Maybe try to get some fish."

So he wouldn't help. "Right," I said, my voice tight.

"Annie and I could probably dig some clams when we're done. We're right there." Mirra was more forgiving than me.

"Great. See you later." He strode off.

As soon as he was out of earshot, I turned to Mirra. "We're going to have to keep our eye on him. I bet he messes up our message."

"He might. He sure is hard to figure out."

I agreed. All I knew for sure was that we should spell out HELP. It could save our lives.

It took Mirra and me until late afternoon, but we finally dragged enough wood to form the letters. Afterward, I brushed the dirt and sand off my hands. The tide was out. Time to get some clams.

While we looked for spout marks, I asked Mirra a question that had been on my mind. "Do you think it's strange Roman didn't want to take the horse hide?"

"Maybe it grossed him out."

"Maybe," I said. "Or maybe he knows he'll be picked up by winter and there's no need for a warm blanket."

Mirra's eyes widened with panic, and I wished I hadn't brought it up. Together, we knelt in the sand, dug, then dug deeper until we pulled up a clam.

My stomach growled, letting me know it'd been a long time since breakfast. I concentrated on finding spout marks. Finally, after wading out to a sandbar, I found a bunch.

"Over here," I called to Mirra.

"How deep is it?" Mirra asked.

"Only to my waist. Be prepared. It's cold."

Mirra splashed in. I handed her the other half of a clam shell as a shovel.

Within a few minutes, we each had a clam. "Not exactly French fries, but they'll fill us up."

I wished Mirra hadn't mentioned French fries. As I dug another clam, my mouth filled with saliva. Ah, the smell of fries sizzling in grease. "The last fries I had were after taking my final math test," I said. "Hailey and I stopped at the diner.

"Hailey seems nice, and she's talented." Mirra added a clam to the pile. I've seen some jewelry she's designed."

"Yeah, she's spending most of the summer with her dad in Wyoming, but she'll be back mid-August." I silently added, *But would we?*

I looked around. The tide had come in. "We have to head back."

Mirra dropped her clam-shovel. "How'd we get so far from shore?"

"The tide came in." I took off the coral jacket, and ignoring the pain in my hand, held it out. "Toss the clams in here and help me tie this around my waist."

It took precious minutes before we'd done that. "Hurry," I said, stepping in the water. "You might have to swim."

"Swim? With this current? I can't!"

"You have to, Mirra. My arm. I can't hold you up and swim too." I kept Mom's fleece tied around my waist, but I let the clams drop back in the water. Seeing what I'd done, Mirra sucked in a breath.

"We have to go." I circled her waist, then led her toward the dark, swirling water. "Remember what Roman taught you?"

"Isn't there another way?"

Was there time for me to swim for shore, find something that would float, or run to get Roman? No, our sandbar was nearly gone.

"It's okay, Annie," Mirra said. "You swim for it. Maybe I'll be okay here."

"I'm not leaving you. We go together. Now!" I grabbed Mirra's hand and squeezed it for courage. Then we plunged in. Within seconds we were over our heads, and it was all I could do to paddle with my one arm and keep myself afloat.

"You okay?" Mirra called to me. Her arm movements were jerky, but she was swimming.

A huge wave pounded me. Off balance, I tumbled under the chilling water. When I finally righted myself and surfaced for a breath, Mirra was searching for me.

Treading water, Mirra called, "Annie?"

I tried gurgling back an answer, but another wave blasted me.

"Paddle. You can do this!"

Before the next wave hit, Mirra was swimming at my side. "Come on," she commanded.

Stroke, kick-kick, stroke, kick-kick. When I felt the sand under my feet, I staggered alongside Mirra. I coughed out water, stumbled toward shore, and fell onto the sand.

"Thank you," I finally said. "Those waves. Blasted me. Couldn't breathe."

"Your wrist," Mirra said, wiping her face. "Is it okay?"

"Hurts." I swept my hair from my face and looked at her. "You swam, Mirra. You did great."

"I ... I did it, didn't I? Wait until we tell Roman."

A new thought struck me. Roman knew we were going to dig clams on the flats. He knew about tides. He knew Mirra couldn't swim well and that I had a hurt wrist. No word of caution. In fact, he'd hurried off leaving us alone.

When we told Roman, I watched his face, but he only appeared proud of Mirra. "Good going. You might have even saved Annie's life."

I watched him out of the corner of my eye for the rest of that day, but I was no closer to figuring him out.

In the morning, Roman came later than usual. He made some excuse about sleeping in, but I wasn't buying it. Could he have messed with our HELP message? As soon as I'd eaten, I said, "I'm off to, uh, look around."

Mirra eyed me suspiciously, but said, "Okay."

I spotted horses in the distance and headed their way. I recognized Sea Stallion. "Are you keeping watch over your mares and yearlings?" I asked from a distance.

He tossed his head.

"Well, I'm keeping watch over Roman. I'll start by checking our *HELP* message."

It took me a while to find the same high flat spot where we'd formed the letters because half the letters weren't readable. Either the wind had been stronger than I thought, or Roman was wrecking our chances to escape this island.

CHAPTER TWENTY-TWO
DEEP HURTS

As I reformed the H-E-L-P letters, a swarm of biting flies descended. I gritted my teeth and got the job done. By the time I got back to camp, my fly bites itched, making my temper rage. How dare that selfish Roman mess with our rescue message. He was selling us out, betraying us. Blood pooled from a bite I'd scratched raw.

Mirra was adding firewood to the pile and Roman was rigging a fishing pole when I declared, "Let's do another Deep Secret."

"O-kay." Mirra stepped close to me.

I tried to keep my tone neutral. "The story of the person who betrayed me."

"I'm taking a pass on this one, ladies." Roman waved his fishing pole and grabbed a bottle of water. "I'm going to kick back with a cold one and try to catch us some fish." He shot us a mischievous smile.

I didn't smile back. After he was out of hearing, I added, "Our HELP message was all messed up."

Mirra spun around to face me. "You think he did it?"

"I don't think the wind was strong enough to move all that driftwood."

"Should we ask him?"

I pictured confronting him, demanding to know if he'd moved the letters. "He might not walk that way for a while and see I fixed them," I said. "I think it'd be better if he doesn't know we're on to him."

"I suppose. It's not like we could make him stop. We'll have to be smarter, or sneakier."

"Exactly."

I took off my splint and used my arm to add wood to the fire. No difference without the splint, I decided, so I returned Mirra's shirt and set the splint in the tent. Spotting Mom's coral fleece, I brought it to where Mirra sat near the fire. "Can we still do the *Dark Secret?*"

She eyed the fleece. Her voice was gentle when she asked, "Do you want to talk about your mom?"

I sat across from her. A tidal wave of emotion built inside, a wave as powerful as the one that had sunk our boat. Mom hadn't meant to leave me, but somehow that didn't help.

A powerful sob came out of my throat that was a tsunami of all the tears I hadn't shed over Mom's death and all the hurt I hadn't let out after Mirra's mean comments and all the worry I'd kept inside about Roman and our survival. My body shook with my sobs. I knew when Mirra squatted down next to me and stroked my back that I was scaring her, but I didn't care.

I cried and cried.

When it was over, I didn't dare look at her. Finally, I said, "I'm sorry. I didn't expect that."

Mirra brought a log over close to me. "Annie, you've been so brave. You've been taking care of us all this time. It's amazing you haven't cried like this before. Tell me."

I couldn't stop my shoulders from shaking. "I ... I haven't told anyone, but I saw the car ...after ...after the accident." *Breathe. Just breathe.* "I snuck into the wreckage yard. The ...the windshield. I saw it." A great sob poured out of me. "And I was mean to her, that last morning. My last words to my mother and they were...they were..."

"I can promise you that your mom knew you loved her," Mirra said gently. She put her arm around my waist and pulled me close. "Don't think about that last morning. Your mom has forgiven you." Mirra wiped a tear from my cheek. "She was always so full of fun. Remember when she rode around on Steven's scooter, laughing the whole time?"

I nodded.

"She'd be so proud of you. For the way you're taking care of the boys—and for this." She motioned toward the fire and shelter. "You've kept us alive."

Mom. Proud of me. I basked in that thought.

A bird twittered in a nearby bush. "Remember how much she loved birds?" I asked.

Mirra nodded.

"Once we were walking in the woods and a white-throated sparrow sang." My voice cracked. "She told me it was her favorite bird."

"If we get back home," Mirra said, "let's set up a bird feeder on her grave. We can keep it filled summer and winter."

I gulped. "That's a nice idea."

"I hope you'll give me another chance," Mirra said, "to be a better friend."

We sat a while longer. "There's a second part to seeing the car."

"What's that?"

"After I saw it, I called a cab and had him drop me off at the guy's house. I'd checked his address days before. My mind wasn't thinking straight. I thought if I saw him, I might shove him or shout at him. But none of that happened.

"His house was tiny and I could see through the picture window. His wife and he were sitting around the kitchen table. They have three young kids and they kept popping in and out. He looked so serious I was sure he was talking about the accident. She looked really sad too. At one point, a small girl crawled on his lap, and he hugged her tight."

"That must have been hard," Mirra said, "to see him."

I swallowed. "You know that he fell asleep at the wheel, right?"

Mirra nodded.

"I'd heard that he had two jobs. I know I was supposed to keep hating him, but after seeing him with his wife and hugging his kid, well, I just couldn't."

It was nearly dark. I stood. Mirra wrapped an arm around my waist. "That's good," she said. "There's enough hate out there."

I let her support me; her strong body like an anchor holding me steady and helping me heal.

* * *

The following morning, Mirra brought me strawberry leaf tea. "How are you doing?" she asked, her eyes lowered.

"Better." I smiled weakly.

I noticed the puffiness around her eyes. I guessed her worries about her skin had kept her up last night.

Roman walked toward us, fishing pole in hand. I realized I'd seen similar shadows under Roman's eyes. Thinking of all he'd done to hurt us, I wasn't surprised.

Our chatter turned to needing to wash out clothes. While Roman fished on one end of the lake, we scrubbed clothes on the other. Ripped and becoming thread-bare, they wouldn't stand too many more washings.

A splashing sound made me turn my head to see Roman pulling in a fish. Mirra and I headed toward a clump of bushes to spread out the newly washed clothes so they could dry. I was checking out the sky for rain clouds when a whirring noise made me freeze. It took a second to register the sound. An engine! Far away but coming our way. "Helicopter!" I screamed.

"Signal fire!" Mirra cried, dropping the wet clothes.

My mind spun. North and east signal fires were closest. We needed to get burning sticks from our campfire. "This way!" I called to Mirra as I ran. "We'll add wood to our campfire first. Build it up. Grab sticks to light the north and east signal fires." Roman! I'd nearly forgotten about him. I could hear the swish of his pant legs as he charged toward us. Would he help us? Or would he snuff out our fires?

Roman's swishing legs shot ahead of me. I lost him in the dunes. By the time I got to our campfire, I was gasping for breath, but I didn't waste a second. The helicopter was nearly above us. I threw more wood on the fire. Mirra panted up alongside. I used the hem of my T-shirt to grab the end of a burning stick. Mirra did the same. "Go!"

The helicopter's whirr kept me focused. Was it too high up to see our HELP message or fires? Mirra and I had to get the other fires blazing or smoking. We ran as fast as we could with the lit sticks. We were nearly to the signal fire when Roman charged toward us, eyes animal-wild, his own burning stick in hand. I raised my stick, ready to attack him.

Roman slowed. He lifted the burning stick. Did he mean to use it as a weapon? He paused. The island seemed to hold its breath along with us.

Roman swung. Toward the pile of firewood. Toward our rescue.

We moved as one, touching our torches to the bits of bark. His flame joined with ours and like hands reaching out to help each other, the blaze rose skyward.

Oh, Roman. Thank you!

The helicopter passed over us. The three of us jumped up and down and waved.

When it continued toward the south shore, Roman ran along with it. I held my breath and prayed, *please God, please, have them see us.* But it kept flying away. Farther and farther away.

I couldn't bring myself to look at Mirra. The roaring waves drowned out the hum of the helicopter.

Mirra's and my cries were softer than they'd ever been. The grueling days of hunger, thirst, blazing sun, whipping wind, cold, and loneliness hadn't left us with enough energy for useless tears.

Roman was standing alongside us a few minutes later when I thought I heard the helicopter's whir again. I looked. Yes! It had swung back around! Our fires sent smoke skyward. Mirra, Roman, and I waved our arms. It was nearly directly overhead. It seemed to pause in midair for agonizingly long seconds, then, hallelujah!

"It's coming down!" I shouted. "Someone saw us!" My heart leaped clear up to my throat. Could it be?

Thank you, Lord. Thank you.

It was low enough now so we could see the official DNR insignia on its side. "Yes!" I shrieked. "Yes! Yes! YES!"

Mirra grabbed my hands, and we jumped around, laughing and squealing and crying at the same time.

The helicopter landed on the beach in a cloud of flying sand. The engine stopped. I held my breath as the silhouette of a single person opened the door. An older man in a green ranger uniform hurried out. He took in our shabby clothes and tangled hair. "What on earth? Are you the missing kids?"

"Yes!" Mirra squealed.

Silly as I must look, I jumped up and down. "We're so glad to see you!"

"I don't believe this! I've been reading about you." The ranger's eyes shifted to face Roman. "But who are you?"

Chapter Twenty-Three
Confession

I hurried over to Roman's side, but he still looked like a spooked horse ready to bolt.

The ranger softened his tone. "Let me start over. I'm Ben, with the Department of Natural Resources. I come every few months to check on the horses. I was just going to fly over when I noticed smoke. I haven't heard about a missing young man. What's your name, son?

"I'm Roman Mar—." He paused a second, slid a gaze at us, and continued. "Roman Macchio."

Ben nodded and then headed to his helicopter. "I'll get on the radio. People are going to be so excited. Come with me. I have some apples inside. It's too bad I don't have room for all three of you, but we'll get the Coast Guard here as soon as possible."

Ben chatted with Roman while Mirra and I squealed, talked, and wiped away tears.

The apple Ben handed me was heavy. His excited voice carried from the helicopter. "I found the lost girls! And a young man!"

While he gave details, I bit into the crispness, remembering the last apple I'd tasted. Mirra and I had fought while on the raft and ended up losing that apple. I wondered if she remembered that too.

Roman didn't eat his. Instead, he stared out at the ocean.

Mirra and I had finished our apples—I had to force myself not to eat the seeds and core—when Ben stepped back out. "Sorry that took so long." He didn't make eye contact with Roman. "A cutter will be here in a couple of hours."

Mirra grinned at me.

"There'll be an EMT onboard to check you out." He turned to me. "I've noticed your wrist. Did you break it?"

"Uh huh, but look at Mirra's arm. That spot keeps growing."

Ben looked. He tried to cover his expression, but his tone let me know he thought this was bad. "We're going to take good care of you," he said gently. He patted Mirra's back and then glanced at the three of us. "You have time to grab anything you want to bring home."

"Is someone calling our parents?" Mirra asked.

"As we speak."

Roman rubbed his right hand on his shorts. Would there be police officers meeting us too?

Ben, a serious expression on his face, walked over to Roman. I wished I could hear what they were saying.

"Come on," Mirra said, pulling on my arm. "Let's get our things. Race you to camp." She shot off ahead.

I jogged after her, but stopped well before camp. I looked around the island. My last day here. Part of me was desperate to leave before something else went wrong, but part of me wanted to soak in every detail. The texture of the sand, the smell of the campfire, and even the taste of saltwater spray on my lips.

I broke into a sprint and arrived at camp behind Mirra. She already held the knife. I remembered how she'd been so matter-of-fact after breaking off its tip, saying, "It's just a knife." Now, using her shirt, she wiped it off carefully. "Can I have this?" she asked.

"Yes."

"I never realized—" she began, then broke off as she went inside our tent.

I gathered up the cookie tin. Joey and Steven might get a kick out of hearing how we'd used it on the raft and later to keep the terns from pecking our heads and to carry water. I noticed the fish Roman had caught earlier, and nearly added it to the tin. I realized I no longer needed to worry about where I would get my next bite of food.

Castaway Island had sheltered Mirra, Roman, and me, and it would continue to be home for the horses. I scooped up a handful of its sand and carefully poured it into the tin. Finally, I tucked the glittery hair clip in my pocket. The day before the shipwreck, I'd held this clip and wished to be more than a girl who'd lost a mother and a best friend, more than a daughter and a big sister needing to keep the family together. I stood tall. I'd gotten my wish.

I looked off toward the dunes and spotted Sea Stallion, the horse that had helped us by leading me to water that first horrible day and had kept my hope alive all these weeks. He stood, watching. *Goodbye*, I silently said. *I hope I see you again.*

"Annie," Mirra whispered after dismantling the tent, "Roman's coming. And something's wrong."

Seeing Roman's slumped shoulders and shadowed eyes, I couldn't help looking frantically to make sure the helicopter was still there. It was. I breathed. "What is it?"

He held out his story stick. "I ... I'd like to tell you something. Can we sit?" He motioned to the sand.

The three of us sat in a close circle. Roman stroked the carved piece of driftwood, which was much more detailed than the last time I'd seen it. He ran his thumb from the carving of the girl, to the mean-looking man, to the fist, to the lifeless man, and finally to the end. He held it so Mirra and I could see the last carving—a figure behind the bars of a jail cell.

"I couldn't say anything before," Roman began, handing me the carved driftwood, "but I want to now. Then you'll know why I didn't show myself to you when you first came, and why I didn't signal the rescue boat." He brought his fingers to his temples and pressed hard, as if he could make a pounding headache go away.

Mirra and I locked eyes.

"This is hard. I've kept it secret for so long. I ... I ... " He rubbed his thumb over the carving of the girl. "I killed someone." He couldn't look at us. "I didn't mean to. It was an accident. Still ... "

Mirra gasped. "Who was it?"

"A creepy older guy my twin was dating." He drew in a long breath. "It was May first. We were alone in the car after celebrating Dad's birthday, when I saw bruises on her arm. I asked about them and she finally told me that the night before Damien had gotten rough with her." The veins stood out on Roman's neck.

"Did she tell your parents?" Mirra asked.

Roman shook his head. "He threatened if she did, he'd come after our thirteen-year-old sister, Miranda, and hurt her. Bad."

He didn't need to go into details. My throat closed in.

"When I heard, I tore off. I knew where the creep lived and headed straight there." He closed his eyes for a second. "Tamara kept pleading with me to turn around, not to let him know she told, but I couldn't. People talk about seeing red. I saw explosions of red." Roman covered his face with his hands. He stayed that way a long time.

I stared at the closed fist on his driftwood. "You punched him?"

Roman nodded, then rubbed the knuckles of his right hand. "I pounded on the door. He answered it, stepping onto the cement stoop. I didn't give him a chance to open his mouth. I punched him in the jaw. He fell back, hit his head. Hard. There was blood ... lots of blood."

Roman's hands shook.

Roman had said he wasn't sure if he believed in heaven, but that he was sure about hell. Things were finally making sense.

"Tamara started screaming," Roman continued. "I was shaking. More from fear than anger now. I bent over him." He swallowed, drew in a breath, and continued. "Heard strange gurgling sounds. Then ... then nothing."

Mirra pressed her knuckles to her mouth and lowered her head.

"Did you call 911?" I asked.

Roman shook his head. "I panicked. Couldn't think straight. The neighbor came outside and called the police. When we heard sirens, Tamara shouted for me to run.

"I ... I did." Roman ran his fingers through his long hair. "I'd killed a man. I was old enough to be tried as an adult. My only thought was to run, so I drove to the marina and hopped in our boat, thinking I'd be hard to trace. More mistakes."

"You can still tell the police what Damien did," Mirra suggested.

"It's not that easy. I murdered someone, then I ran away." He stared out at the ocean.

"So that's why you let the rescue boat leave," Mirra murmured. "You didn't want the police to find you and put you in jail."

He nodded.

I set the driftwood story stick on the sand.

"I'm sorry I didn't signal your parents' boat when they came. The thought of spending the rest of my life in jail was just so..." He left the thought hanging.

"Did you also mess with our HELP message?"

"No, the wind must have done that. I decided a while ago, about the time of the last cold spell, that if another rescue boat came, I'd help. I couldn't cause your deaths too."

I tried to wrap my head around this. "Roman," I began, "you said you saw us when we first landed. Did you know how weak we were?"

"No, I saw your fire that night and figured you'd be okay. Mirra told me a few days ago how close you'd come to dying. I didn't know." He stared at his knuckles. "I've messed up so many times."

"Maybe," Mirra said, "but we'll make sure the police know how much you helped us too." She cocked her head. "How did you wind up on this island?"

"I headed out, not sure where I was going." Roman ran his thumb along the sharp etchings on the story stick. "The gas tanks were full when I started, but once the gauge registered half full, I had to figure out something." He looked off to sea. "By the time I spotted this place, I was running on fumes. The waves were calm, so I trolled close to it. When I saw the horses, I figured there must be fresh water, so I threw out the anchor.

"As soon as it got light enough to see, I inflated the raft that was onboard and threw everything that I could into it. I had to get rid of the boat so I used the ax to punch a hole in the bottom and hull. When it started to sink, I jumped into the raft and paddled to shore."

Roman swayed back and forth. "Less than an hour after I landed, I heard a search plane. They came once more, and twice a patrol boat stopped to look, but I hid in the grass." He pointed. "That patch over there." He handed me the story stick.

I turned it over. On the opposite side, he'd carved a detailed image of splinted-arm me carrying a tin of water and another of Mirra thrashing her arms in the pond.

"And this carving?" Mirra leaned over and pointed to a rectangle shape.

"It's an eraser." He gave a bitter laugh. "If only it was that simple."

Ben appeared. I sensed he'd been watching us. "I see the cutter."

I looked out on the horizon. Sure enough, a flashing white blob was getting bigger. I caught Roman's expression. Fear, yes, but something else too. He looked resigned. Calm.

"Do you have your things?" Ben asked.

I grabbed the tin. "Roman?" I asked.

"This is all I need." He picked up his story stick.

I glimpsed Muscle Boy trotting up a dune. "He's not nearly as good looking as Sea Stallion."

"Sea Stallion?" Ben asked.

"That's the name I gave the dark one with patches of silver."

"Ah, yes. The one with the white crescent moon on its forehead. There's something special about that one."

"Why are the horses here?" I asked.

"People brought them over from Europe in the late eighteenth century. Later, they brought others to improve the breeding stock. The Canadian government protects them, and I help watch over them."

"We found a horse carcass," Mirra told Ben, "and a human skeleton too. Right next to it were musket balls, a shoe buckle, and old coins." Mirra looked toward me. "I should go get those too." She trotted off.

"Well, isn't that something!" Ben said, glancing at me. "You three had a lot of excitement." He glanced at his watch. "I need to make a few rounds to check on things. Be right back."

After he left, I tried to make sense of my connection with Sea Stallion. When I saw Roman's face, though, my thoughts turned to him. I hurried over to his side. "It'll be okay," I said, gently. "We'll tell the police how you saved Mirra from drowning, how you taught us to fish, and figured out how to make fire.

We probably wouldn't be alive without you. That has to count for something."

He raised his eyebrows and shrugged. Then he put his brotherly arm around me and held me close.

* * *

A middle-aged man in a navy blue cap and uniform lowered a small yellow boat off of the side of the cutter. Soon he, along with a police officer, steered toward where the four of us stood on shore. Roman shifted from foot to foot. When he'd finished running his hands through his hair for the third time, he brought his arms to his sides. His hands trembled.

"Hello," the pilot called. His search and rescue vest bore the words *US Coast Guard*. He threw out the anchor, stepped out, and waded toward us, the other man behind. "I'm Petty Officer Martinez and this is Officer Riley."

The police officer nodded at Mirra and me briefly, but he kept his gaze mostly on Roman. "We'll have a chance to talk later when your parents and a lawyer are present."

Roman seemed to shrink into himself.

"Is anyone in immediate need of care?" the petty officer asked.

We all shook our heads. Mirra said, "We just want to go home."

Home.

Ben waved to us. "I'll leave you in the Coast Guard's expert hands," he said. "Goodbye for now. Good luck to you."

I hugged him tight. "Thank you." My voice choked, and it took a moment before I could continue. "Watch over the horses for me, especially Sea Stallion."

"You can count on it."

Mirra and Roman said their goodbyes too, and Ben strode to his helicopter.

Mirra stepped into the small, yellow boat. Roman followed. I scanned the waves telling myself there was no reason to panic. Still, it took a minute to find the nerve. I clutched the side as we motored away from shore.

As we neared the cutter displaying an American flag, a young woman in a blue cap and uniform waved to us from the huge deck.

"We're going home in style," Mirra said.

The cutter was at least three times the size of *Buried Treasures*. Its chrome side rails were so shiny I had to blink. The police officer helped Mirra from the swaying boat to the ladder. She waved to me from the cutter's deck.

Roman motioned for me to go next. Instead of thinking about falling in or the waves, I kept my eye focused on the officer's outstretched hand.

The woman helped me step from the ladder to the deck. Once Roman joined us on board, she said, "I'm Seaman Carol, just Carol will do, and that's Captain

Brian at the helm." An older man waved. While the crew dealt with the small boat, Carol said, "You've been stranded on an island since spring?"

Mirra and I nodded. I kept staring at her moist lips. Did I have enough guts to ask if she had any lip balm?

Petty Officer Martinez joined us. "Welcome aboard." He pointed. "Head to the galley and get out of the sun."

I let everyone else go ahead of me. Then, I took one last look at the island. Parts of the dunes were purple shadows, others were soft yellows.

I wondered if someday the three of us would return.

"Come on, Annie," Mirra called. "They have food for us."

Food! I turned and followed the others.

Chapter Twenty-Four
Reunion

Mirra, Roman, and I followed Carol. The cutter had picked up speed, and the sway made me grab for the rail. "Careful," she warned. "You don't have your sea legs yet."

This struck Mirra and I as funny, and we giggled.

"You have about two hours before we dock," she continued. "The medic needs to check you over."

A fifth stranger, an older woman, finished with Roman quickly. When Mirra asked if she'd see the two of us together, she agreed. My wrist and the mark on Mirra's arm caused her to ask a bunch of questions. "I can't tell if it's broken or not," she said to me, "but you'll get X-rays soon. For now, let me wrap it for you."

Turning to Mirra she said, "The mark does look like skin cancer to me. A specialist will be waiting at the dock. He or she will take care of you. It's good you didn't have to let it go any longer."

When we rejoined Carol and Roman, she was giving him a tour. "And this is the head." She opened a door. A toilet, shower, bars of soap, towels, and a sink with faucets. I grinned at Mirra. A turn of the knob and water would pour out. Water!

"Ready for drinks and a light sandwich?" Carol smiled.

The galley had a microwave, refrigerator, and a huge sink. "We have sodas and juices and sandwich fixings," she offered. "Ham, turkey, lettuce, and cheese." When she opened the refrigerator, I gasped, unable to contain myself.

"We have juice or ice tea or water of course," Carol said. "What can I get you?"

I couldn't get my mouth to work. Finally I stammered, "Water."

She handed me a clear glass filled to the top. I took a swallow. Then another. I gulped it down.

She asked us insane questions like whether we preferred mayo or mustard, sweet or dill pickles, American or Swiss cheese.

When I saw the three white plates, each with pickles, chips, and a sandwich, I collapsed onto the bench next to Mirra. Roman slid in alongside me.

The wonderful smells made me light-headed and giddy. Carol handed me a linen napkin. I held the cloth to my face. Luxury.

Mirra, Roman, and I picked up our sandwiches at the same time. The bread smelled nutty and sweet. I tried to make it last in my mouth. Impossible. I wanted to wolf down the whole thing. Afterward, I excused myself to use the bathroom.

"Take a shower if you want," Carol said. "We keep extra toothbrushes, combs, and lotion in there.

Help yourself to anything you see. Let me grab a few T-shirts from my rack."

She returned with three T-shirts. "Thanks," I said. We each took one. I used the toilet and flushed for the first time since early June. I caught sight of myself in the mirror. Oh my God! Straggly hair and leathery, blotchy skin. Shaken, I shed my clothes and stepped into the shower. I uncapped the coconut shampoo and massaged my scalp. I held a dollop of soap to my nose and practically purred. "Mmmm." I soaped my arms, legs, and body. I let the warm water soothe my tired muscles and dry skin. After I toweled off, I caught sight of myself in the mirror a second time.

I combed out my hair, then opened a bottle of lotion. I poured some on my hands and gently rubbed a generous amount onto my leathery arms. These were the arms that had helped carry Mirra onto the island. I rubbed lotion into my legs. Without these strong legs, I could never have found us water or gathered firewood. Finally, I rubbed Vaseline onto my lips, and lotion onto my face, forehead, and my feet. Spearing fish, capturing and cooking a duck, and roasting seal meat would have been impossible without this body. I looked in the mirror again. This time, I didn't see scars or peeling skin. I only saw a strong, beautiful body. A body that had survived.

Chin high, shoulders back, I returned to Mirra and Carol. Roman must be on deck. "The pie's warm," Carol said. "Would you like a little with ice cream?"

"Yes, please," I said.

I let the warmed apples and cold ice cream sit on my tongue until I had to swallow. "Mmm," I moaned.

"This is so good," Mirra seconded.

"Captain Brian here," a voice rang through the speaker system. "We'll be docking in thirty minutes. Officers will try to shield you from the press, but I want to warn you, they'll be shouting out questions."

"Maybe we'll be on TV!" Mirra licked a final dribble of apple pie from her lips. "Come on. I'll do your hair."

Mirra and I scooted back into the bathroom. She brushed and then French-braided my hair before doing her own, which still had some of the purplish colors from her last trip to the salon. "Now let's bring this brush to Roman."

We found Roman standing outside by the bow. The sun was low in the sky. "Want me to fix your hair?" Mirra said.

He bent at the knees so it was easier for her to work. "There!" she declared soon after. "Now you look like the all-American boy."

Roman smiled, but when he spoke, it was with a serious tone. "I'd like to tell you goodbye."

I frowned. "We'll see each other."

"I'm not sure they'll allow visitors where I'm going, and even if they did, your parents won't like their daughters visiting a guy in jail."

No, I realized, they wouldn't. "We aren't saying goodbye. We're sticking by you and finding a way to keep in touch."

"Roman?" Officer Riley's badge caught the light and made me blink.

"Coming, sir." Roman joined the officer.

I tried to swallow, but there was a huge lump in my throat.

Minutes later, Carol handed Mirra binoculars. "Check it out."

"I think I see land and cars! Oh-my-gosh! I see people. I think I see my mom ... and Dad!" Her sun-weathered face broke out into a grin.

Roman and the officer joined us. "Look!" She handed me the binoculars, but I passed them to Roman.

"Thanks."

The captain throttled down. Roman adjusted the lenses. "My parents," he said. "I see them. And there's Miranda. And Tamara." He handed me the binoculars and turned away quickly to hide his face.

My hands shook, but I concentrated on holding the binoculars steady. Yellow tape kept a mob of people back. People! Dozens of people. Standing apart was a statuesque woman. It had to be Roman's mother. Dark hair swept up in an elaborate do, she was patting it as if protecting it from the wind. A man with olive skin, who stood closest to her, pressed against the yellow tape, as if he couldn't wait to cross it.

I focused the binoculars in on Mirra's parents talking to two boys. I sucked in air. My brothers. Tears welled in my eyes. I swiped at them quickly, wanting desperately to see. Steven's shorter haircut looked good. Joey turned my way. Seeing him, my heart went up to my throat. And then ... Dad! It was really him. Even though I knew he couldn't hear, I returned the binoculars to Carol, cupped my hands, and shouted. "Dad!" My voice felt powerful enough to carry over the water and meet him.

While people hurried to dock the boat, I soaked in the sight of my family.

Minutes later, Captain Brian said, "Watch your step."

"Thank you!" I exclaimed to the crew. Mirra leaped off the boat and I ran right behind her, down the pier, to the yellow tape. The policemen moved the tape aside and then I was hugging Dad with my good arm and he was crying.

"It's so good to—" Dad choked up too much to continue.

"Welcome back, sis," Steven said, joining the circle.

"Annie!" Joey said, squeezing me around the waist. "I kept telling everyone you weren't dead. I missed you."

"I've missed you too." I didn't care that tears were streaming down my face.

Moments blurred as people in uniforms talked to my father and then directed me toward an ambulance. "Honey, they just told me about your arm. The boys and I will meet you at the hospital."

"Okay, Dad."

The EMTs led me to the back of an ambulance. They were about to shut the door when I shouted, "Wait!" I desperately searched for Mirra. She was wrapped in the arms of her mom and dad. I watched until the three of them headed for a second ambulance.

The EMT wanted to close the door, but I still had to find Roman. I prayed he wouldn't be in handcuffs. When I spotted him, the police were a distance away. The setting sun lit up a girl's joyous face. Tamara! A smiling dad, with his arm around Roman's back, steered his son safely through the crowd. His mother, arm around a younger daughter, who must be Miranda, followed behind.

"Miss," the male EMT said, "we need to assess you."

I moved back, and he closed the door, shutting off my view of my family, Roman, and Mirra. What would they tell Mirra about the spot on her arm? I had a sudden panicky feeling. The vibration from the motor revving up and the squeeze from the blood pressure cuff added to my anxiety. An older woman reminding me of my grandmother held my hand while the male EMT poked and prodded. Just a bit longer, I told myself, and my family and I will be together. Forever.

"We're taking you to the clinic for X-rays," the older EMT said, "but we'll hurry you through. Your dad is meeting us there."

Minutes later, I was walking on pavement and then felt air conditioning. A male nurse ushered me into a bright exam room. The lights made me squint, and I kept shivering. He brought me a warmed blanket and Dad covered me with it. He stroked my cheek and kept patting my back. Throughout the exam and endless questions, he squeezed my hand and stared at me as if he couldn't believe I was really here.

When the nurse led me to get X-rays, Dad kissed my forehead and said, "I'll meet you back in the waiting room."

Somewhere, a nurse or doctor was also examining Roman and Mirra. I let my mind drift toward the future. I wasn't sure what would happen with Roman, but I could predict how things would go with Mirra. We'd be tight—for a while. We'd share the limelight, probably get interviews about our ordeal, but eventually that attention would fade. Mirra would shop and go to parties and get the coolest phone/clothes/boyfriends. Over time, she might still choose boys and the Brittany's of the world over me. And that was okay. Yes, Mirra and I would drift apart at times, but we'd always be deep friends, the kind who would be there for one another in rough patches.

At high school graduation, we'd stand for a picture, maybe not best friends, but friends who will endure.

"All done," the X-ray technician said.

Once I finished with the exam and met Dad and my brothers in the waiting room, Dad wore a pained expression. "What's wrong?" I asked.

"Oh," he rubbed his forehead, "I just found out from the Coast Guard that you were on one of the islands we checked. The one we didn't stay on long because of the foggy weather. If only we would have—"

"It's not your fault, Dad." Someday I'd tell him how Mirra and I had been fighting, and that Roman had seen them but never called out.

The nurse whisked me into the room. She patted my hand. "The doctor said we have to schedule a surgery for your wrist. It was broken and has healed, but it's not straight." She went into details about appointments at my hometown clinic and pain medication if I needed it, but it was hard to concentrate until she said, "You can go home for now."

I shot to my feet.

Joey took my good hand. As soon as the outside door opened, the officer motioned for us to hurry. I was glad for the darkness as reporters shouted out questions and cameras flashed.

"How did you manage to survive?" a woman shouted.

"Tell us about Roman," a man called out. "Did he hurt you at all?"

"No," I answered back quickly, not wanting to ignore this question. "Roman helped us. He saved our lives."

The officer shielded me until I was near the van. "Go in back," Steven called. I sat in the middle and had a brother on each side.

"It's a long drive home," Dad said, after he'd pulled onto a main road. "We could stay at a hotel. Do you want to stop for something to eat?"

"I'm not hungry, and I'd rather head home if you're okay to drive."

"I'm wide awake," Dad said. "How are you doing? Does your wrist hurt?"

"Only a little. The quiet is nice."

"Annie," Joey said, bouncing on the seat, "I've been wanting to tell you. There'll be a surprise at home."

"Oh? What is it?"

"I'm not telling." By his grin, though, I could guess.

"I've been making suppers," Steven said out of the blue.

"He's doing a great job," Dad said. "Wait until you try his special omelets."

Steven beamed.

"Is Ryan still at the house?" I asked.

"No, he's back home. He and Uncle Jim spent days searching for you too. I called Jim and Grandma and Grandpa while you were getting your X-rays so they know what's happening. I'm not sure we can keep them away tomorrow, but I can try. You need to rest."

Joey snuggled into me and yawned. He soon fell asleep.

Steven said, "You can go to sleep against me if you want."

I blinked in surprise. My brother, the one who I couldn't get to shower and had been making breakfast for, was taking care of me. I rested my head on his shoulder and soon fell asleep.

I awoke to hear Dad's soft voice. "We're home," he said. "Go back to sleep."

But when I stepped into the kitchen and a black and white puppy greeted me, I knew it would be a while before I'd go to bed. I rubbed the soft head.

Joey rubbed his eyes and grinned. "This is Patches."

The puppy wiggled his butt, wagged his tail, and licked my hand. "Joey, he's adorable."

"He usually sleeps with me, but I'll let you take him if you want."

"That's okay," I said, "but I'd sure like to play with him tomorrow. I'd also like to tell you the story of a special stallion living on the island. It had a crescent moon marking on its forehead."

"Really?" Dad said. "How funny. Your mom talked about a neighbor when she was growing up who had a stallion that she loved. It had a half-moon on its forehead. There's a picture of them around someplace. I'll dig it out sometime for you."

Patches headed to the door. "I better take him outside," Joey said. "Hailey and her mom took care of him tonight. They're really nice."

My little brother put a leash on Patches and walked out in the dark.

"Do you want me to make you some food?" Dad asked. "Maybe some pancakes and bacon?"

I shook my head, seeing how he needed to sleep. "No, I'm still full from all I ate on the boat. I just want to go to bed."

After long hugs, I walked into my bedroom, changed into pajamas smelling strangely of laundry detergent, pulled back my comforter, and lay down on the soft sheets. I didn't wake until mid-morning.

I immediately asked Dad if he'd heard anything about Mirra.

"Yes, her mom called. They wouldn't let her leave and performed surgery right away. They believe they got it all. You can find out details later. Right now know that she should be fine."

My legs wobbled.

"I'm making you a breakfast fit for a queen." Dad made bacon, pancakes and pale-colored chicken eggs, nothing like the richer tern eggs I was used to, but my body burst with gratitude. After breakfast, with my dad and brothers gathered around, I began my story by telling about riding the inflatable boat, and landing on the island. I told them how the horse with the crescent moon had led me to water. Dad swallowed, then left to wipe his eyes. He returned with a photo. When I saw it, I gasped.

Mom, looking to be around my age, stood with a horse that looked remarkably like Sea Stallion. Same dark and silvery color, and a crescent moon on its forehead. I looked at my dad. His eyes had filled back up. Someday I hoped to understand all of this, but for now, I was too overwhelmed to think it through.

I took breaks from talking to play with Patches, and to answer Mirra's call. She and I talked for almost an hour about her surgery, how strange it was to ride in a car, have clean clothes, hot and cold water from the faucet, and how hard it was to handle all the noise. People talking, music, and the roar of traffic.

For supper, Hailey and her mom brought over lasagna. "We don't want to intrude," Hailey's mom said, but I convinced them to stay a few minutes.

Hailey gave me a long hug, and I hugged her back. It felt so good.

"Man, that had to be rough," Hailey said, after we'd stepped apart. "I'm so glad you made it. I never believed that you hadn't." She smiled at me. "I told everyone if anyone could survive, it was you."

I filled in details and told them the story of finding the skeleton and the old coins.

"That's so cool," Hailey said. "I'm going to Google it. I bet I'll find out the history. I'll call you when I do."

Shortly after they left, and we'd eaten, the landline rang. Dad's voice sounded guarded. He handed me the phone. "It's Roman."

My hand trembled as I held it to my ear. Was he calling from a jail cell? Did they let prisoners do that? "Roman, where are you?"

"I'm still home. Annie, Damien didn't die! He was just knocked out. It's so incredible. I thought for sure I'd killed him. I've had police interviews and talked to a lawyer. Annie, they haven't charged me. It helps that Damien has a record. I won't have to go to jail!'"

"Oh, Roman, that's wonderful! Have you told Mirra yet?"

"No, I wanted to tell you first."

We talked about Mirra's cancer and my needing surgery. "It's so strange being back in the real world." Roman laughed. "Mom took me into a store to get some stuff, and I had to leave. It was too much."

"Uh-huh. I get that."

"So I'm wondering if you and Mirra would meet me tomorrow so we can talk. I could drive there."

"I'll be here. I'll give you Mirra's number."

After I did, Roman said, "Okay, hope to see you tomorrow." He laughed. "I kind of miss you."

I missed him too. I said goodbye and set down the phone. I looked at the top of my dresser where I'd set the hair clip. I picked it up, turning it so it caught the light and shone. Someday ...

A few minutes later, Mirra sent me a text. "Talked to Roman. Meeting tomorrow at noon. Okay?"

"OK."

I checked in with Dad and then stepped outside into the fading light. After reaching the shoreline, I took off my sandals to feel the still-warm sand. I waded in. The waves were calm tonight. A tern flew overhead, then plunged into the ocean. Mouth empty, it flew east. Who knew? It could be flying toward Castaway Island.

I too, felt pulled toward the island and its mysteries. I would go back someday, I decided. Maybe Roman and Mirra would want to come along, or Ben might let me help keep track of the wild horses.

More terns circled. One of them made a dive. Success! It flew toward me as if it wanted to show off the shiny fish dangling from its beak.

I waved to it.

After finding a large patch of sand, I scooped up a handful. I let it swish through my fingers. *Home*, it sang. *Home.*

THE END

Author's Note

A n author wants her story to come to life for its readers. Research is one way to do this, which explains why I forced myself to eat a raw oyster and why I studied the fresh seafood case so long the clerk nearly called security. Falling off my horse and breaking my arm were real-life experiences I would have been happy to miss, but it did make it easier for me to visualize the hardships Annie faced after her fall.

I based *Stranded on Castaway Island* on a real place. Sable Island is about 100 miles southeast of Nova Scotia. It's shaped like a half moon and earned the nickname "The Graveyard of the Atlantic." Its treacherous, unpredictable currents have claimed many lives. Similar to Annie, Mirra, and Roman, Sable Island explorers uncovered the skeleton of a young man along with a shoe buckle, lead musket balls, and British coins dated 1760. The cause of the young man's death will most likely remain a mystery. Wild horses continue to roam freely through the dunes of Sable Island, and stallions still keep watch over the creatures that inhabit it.

ABOUT THE AUTHOR

Amy Laundrie is the author of *Laugh, Cry, Reflect: Stories from a Joyful Heart* and twelve books for young readers. She enjoys spending time with family and friends, hiking with her beloved dog, playing tennis and pickleball, and walking the beach where she can imagine seeing more of Annie, Mirra, Roman, and Sea Stallion.

Please visit her website, www.laundrie.com for updates and appearances.